monsoonbooks

T0097180

SAMARANG HOTEL

John Webb is a South African author. He has contributed to *Esquire* and *GQ* magazines and his most recent novel, *Nine Letters*, was published by Penguin Random House in 2020. John lived in Laos for six years before moving to the US. He is currently based in Honolulu.

Praise for *Samarang Hotel*

'What Webb does well is balance philosophical questions with humour through the stories of flawed but basically decent people. The themes touched on in *Samarang Hotel* – facing death, the nature of civility, the importance of symbols and myth, and redemption – could be heavy-going without the levity ... an enjoyable book.' John Ross, *Asian Review of Books*

'A moving and unflinching exploration of mystery and mortality set against the beautiful backdrop of Laos, and making room for spy-caper high-jinks.' Rosie Milne, *Asian Books Blog*

Other books by the author

Lotto
Nine Letters

Samarang Hotel

John Webb

monsoon

monsoonbooks

First published in 2021
by Monsoon Books Ltd
www.monsoonbooks.co.uk

No.1 The Lodge, Burrough Court, Burrough on the Hill,
Leicestershire LE14 2QS, UK.

ISBN (paperback): 9781912049868
ISBN (ebook): 9781912049875

Cover design by Cover Kitchen.

A Cataloguing-in-Publication data record is available from the British
Library.

Printed and bound in Great Britain by Clays Ltd, Elcograf S.p.A.
23 22 21   1 2 3

For Tia

The world of the so-called normal, he suspected,
was perhaps even more in need of healing
than the abnormal, because it was in command of the day.

JUNG & The Story of Our Time
Laurens van der Post, 1975

1

I smoke.

It helps to fill in the empty spaces.

But sometimes it's more than that. Sometimes I smoke with the firm and deliberate intention of contracting cancer.

It's not as bad as it sounds. The plan is to stock up on the most powerful painkiller known to humankind. I'll stock by the bucket-load. The truck-load. The shipping-container-load. Whatever it takes.

Even if it's illegal. I'll seek respite and smoke myself to death.

It will seem like one of those unfortunate, but conventional endings. Yet no one will know how deliberately executed it was – by my own hand, my own stained fingers.

I'll fade away. It'll be unremarkable.

For the moment I'm watching TV. And I'm boozed. I could – with a groan – lean over the side of the bed and count the number of empty beer cans on the floor. But I won't bother. Maybe too many. Maybe not enough.

It's a B-grade movie and it's been going on for some time. It's getting near the end.

She, the girl in the movie, says to him, the guy in the movie: 'Jake, no! Stop! Don't do it!'

Jake looks at her, as if from afar, almost incomprehensibly.

He lowers the barrel of the pistol so that it no longer points at his gullet. It's a hopeless situation. He's a hero mistaken for a villain. A good man. A wanted man. The police in bulletproof vests have surrounded the building. They're deposited onto the roof by helicopters. Armed to the teeth. They'll stop at nothing. The captain is bellowing at him from outside, through a loudhailer. Give yourself up, he is saying.

Jake looks again at the girl. 'Oh, yeah?' he says. 'And why not? Tell me why not.'

I laugh out loud. 'Yes, lady! Tell him! Tell Jake why he shouldn't blow his fucking brains out! Come on!' I implore her. '*Tell him!*'

So, she does. She brushes her fringe away from her forehead and she says: 'Because Jake ... because you've got to see how the story ends.'

I'm silenced. Jake is silenced.

I can't stand it another minute.

There's nothing more to be done. I fling my full beer can at the screen. It cracks. It sparks. It glowers at me in rainbowish hues.

I quickly run to unplug it. Don't want to cause a fire.

The following morning I'm at my desk, looking at my computer screen. My eyeballs feel bruised; can't take the white pixelated light. It's a familiar pain. I rub my temples with my fingers and blink at the screen. Memories of the B-grade movie and the broken TV of the night before still linger – make me feel a bit sick.

The computer screen tells me that an Australian banking

group is hosting a lunch in the private dining room – the Orchid Room. That'll go on. Australians have a tendency to make the most of a free lunch.

The World Bank is hosting a workshop in the Bougainvillea Room. The keynote speaker is an economist from Prague. The head of the World Bank mission will be there too. I know her. She's from Ghana.

And this evening it's the Germans in the Fuchsia Room. The ambassador. The NGO crowd. Do-gooders. Hangers on. It's the launch of the Hands-of-Help programme. Fuck them. I yawn. Hands-of-Help! Sounds like a circle jerk to me. I think myself to be amusing.

And what of the guest rooms? I scan through the list. No one exceptional. An American couple. An Englishman who works for a forestry company. A delegation of Korean real estate developers. A Russian. An Indian. An Irishman. A French couple with two kids. That'll be a breeze.

And then there's the name of a woman who appears to come from nowhere. According to the screen, she has no nationality. Nancy Bacon. What a ludicrous name! Wasn't there a famous Bacon? Francis Bacon? Who was he? A poet? An explorer? A painter? One of those people who was *good at everything*? I've never trusted people like that. Too damn full of themselves.

Bacon! Perhaps it's a married name. Marrying a man called Bacon! That's a misstep one way or another.

Jacques walks in. 'Morning!' he says. 'Busy day ahead.'

Cheerful little prick.

In fact, he's so cheerful I wonder if he's really French. He'll grow out of it. They all do. The French sooner than most. The kid's only twenty-nine.

'Yes, a busy day,' I agree.

'The German ambassador rang about tonight.'

'Oh.'

'He wants to know if everything's arranged.'

'Oh.'

'I told him we're all set.'

'Right.'

Jacques looks at me expectantly. He wishes I was more conversational. 'He says he wants to talk to you. Wasn't willing to take my word for it.'

That's me!

People – important people – when they don't want to take another person's word for it, they phone me. They double-check. They reassure themselves. If they want to dot all the 'i's' and cross all the 't's', I am the one they call.

Just so you know, I am, *as it happens*, the manager – the *general* manager – of the Samarang Hotel. Not one of the duty managers, not the food and beverage manager, not the events manager, but the *general* manager – the very apex of power, here at the Samarang Hotel!

The hotel brochure tells me that the Samarang opened its celebrated doors in 1926. A Dutch fellow by the name of Brunner headed over here from Java and built the hotel just across the road from a four-hundred-year-old Buddhist stupa. There are a few old, grainy black-and-white photographs of the original building hanging up in the lobby. It was an ornate, elaborate colonial edifice designed to withstand the ages. But it didn't withstand the ages. The whole thing burned down; was reduced to a smouldering heap in 1950. A French entrepreneur rebuilt the place, relying heavily on the fiercely geometric architectural style of the era: bifurcated staircase in the lobby made of concrete slabs suspended on steel rods from the ceiling. Air-brick along the corridors. Terazzo floors. It was, for many years, feted as the most modern building in town. The first building with an elevator!

It was abandoned during the revolution in 1975. Stripped of furnishings and fittings, wine cellar drained. Crockery carted away. For a time it housed officials from a government department.

Things get a bit vague at this point. The brochure doesn't say much about how the hotel landed up in the hands of Mr Lim – a man of Chinese origin, fluent in French and a decorated veteran of the American war in Vietnam. Somehow, Mr Lim embodies some kind of unmentionable political compromise.

Anyhow, it's a hotel once again! Reopened in 1989 and resumed its place as the most prestigious address in Vientiane – supplier of sumptuous air-conditioned accommodations and fine dining.

The Australian luncheon in the Orchid Room has progressed well into the afternoon – just as I had expected. It's a farewell party for the retiring CEO of the bank. Most of the attendees have already left – discreetly slipped away, but the CEO is still there, accompanied by four of his loyal minions. They're all sozzled, surrounded by empty chairs.

The CEO is so pleased to see me, he's almost tearful.

'Julian!'

'Brian.'

'Jesus, it's good to see you! Come and have a drink with us! Come on, pull up a chair, mate!'

But it's clear that the party has already entered its maudlin death spiral. He looks at me with slightly disturbing eagerness, as if I might salvage him from the cusp of despair.

'Can't, I'm afraid. Still on duty. Just thought I'd pop in and say hi.'

'Well how's that for timing? I'm retired now. On my bike, mate. Heading home!'

'That's true,' I reply. 'Just popped in to say bye, I suppose.'

They all laugh uproariously. They think I'm enormously funny. I love the way booze does that.

I make an appearance at the World Bank workshop during their afternoon tea-break. I've never understood why they call these things 'workshops'. They don't *look* like workshops. They all seem so bored, like they're having a day off.

'Susan, so lovely to see you.'

Susan is the head of the World Bank mission. The Ghanaian.

'Hello, Julian. Thanks as always.' She looks around and notes how the workshop delegates are all enjoying animated conversations over tea and pastries – served by unstintingly polite staff in ironed uniforms with gold buttons. That's me. I did that.

'Oh, it's no bother,' I say.

Susan introduces me to the economist from Prague – the keynote speaker. I smile at him broadly. He grunts sourly. He wants to get back to the 'workshop'. Eastern Europeans. I've never been sure about them. They all seem so skittish.

The point is I know everyone in this town. Everyone *worth* knowing, that is. There are plenty of people not worth knowing. Believe me. But I know the ones that count. The ambassadors, the ministers of state, the heads of missions, the country directors, presidents of the chambers of commerce. I know them all. And they know me. And we all get along swimmingly. Swimmingly!

And when I say that I know all the people that count, what I mean is that I like them and they like me. We're always drinking together, conversing over delectable canapés, occasionally back-slapping each other in the sumptuous function rooms of the Samarang.

That evening I pop in to the launch of the Hands-of-Help project, hosted by the German government in the Fuchsia Room – the largest and most resplendent function room of the hotel. The ambassador I know well. I call him Kurt. He calls me Julian. He's giving his welcome speech. His wife, a glossy blonde, her hair piled up elaborately on her head stands next to him, nodding and smiling.

I stand at the back of the Fuchsia Room. I've taken a glass of Gewurztraminer. It's suitably chilled. But I don't listen to Kurt. I never listen to the speeches. They're all the same. Worse than infomercials. Germany is the best. It's done great things. It truly cares. Well ... we all know that old story. Not that I should single out the Germans, poor sods. They all do it. Like they're selling some kind of product.

I look around the room. Who else is here? I look at the backs of their heads as they face the podium.

There's the U.S. *chargé d'affaires*. Leeza or Leena or

something like that. I know her. She knows me. And there's the Indian first secretary. Rajesh. A joker! I like him too. There's Walter, the head of the European Chamber of Commerce – an opinionated little prick, I'll tell you, but we get along. And Erika, the deputy representative of the EU delegation. There are local superstars too. Officials. Budding tycoons. I know them all. I have to admit that the names of the local dignitaries tend to escape me. Unpronounceable, most of them.

Kurt doesn't make eye contact with me while he speaks. Then again, I'm standing at the back of the room. I'm one of two hundred people. I can hardly be expected to hold that against him. And yet ... I am tall and most of the people in the room are Asian so, you know, I am – for wont of a better word – noticeable.

Kurt's speech comes to an end. Germany has never looked this good. Everyone claps, including me. People turn to each other and begin talking. I stand in elegant isolation at the back of the room, but I'm hardly anxious. This is my turf. Someone will make eye contact eventually. They'll pop over. We'll have a bit of pointless conversation. I am, after all, the general manager and we all get along swimmingly.

Next thing I know, Kurt is standing right in front of me. The ambassador himself!

'Kurt!'

He looks at me with such intensity I can't quite tell what he's after. Embrace me or berate me.

'Julian. The Gewurztraminer!' he blanches.

'Delicious,' I say with a winning smile.

'It's warm!'

'Warm?'

I look at my glass, turn it this way and that.

'*Ja*. It's quite warm. I mean, *come on*! You know, this isn't acceptable.'

I almost get the feeling that I'm being drawn into the midst of a particularly prickly international incident. I can see the ticker tape on CNN:

BKNG NEWS: WINE WOES AT SAMARANG THREATEN WORLD PEACE

This is a plainly catastrophic situation. I spring into action. I look at Kurt with an urgency that startles him. 'Kurt. Leave it to me.'

He's hardly convinced.

I snap my fingers. I'm instantly surrounded by staff members in tunics.

'Get the Gewurztraminer onto ice!'

They all run off and do just that – bless their cotton socks.

I leave the Fuchsia Room – the tips of my ears are a fuchsia hue. I rapidly smoke two cigarettes in quick succession.

Did I happen to mention that Kurt – the German Ambassador – is a cunt?

I don't think I did.

But we all get along swimmingly.

2

It's after 9 pm and I am needed to solve a crisis.

A crisis is a rare thing at the Samarang Hotel. But when we encounter one, there is no one in the building who is more eminently empowered to resolve it than me.

The night manager, an effeminate Nepalese man called Farr, is standing at the door to my room. He is so pale I tell him that he looks as if he's seen a ghost. 'It's worse than a ghost,' he says.

I splash my face and dress hurriedly: crisp white shirt, silk grey tie, black trousers, black jacket and shiny black shoes. This is how I face the world, seven days a week.

I advance down the corridor with my heels clicking dramatically on the terrazzo floors. Farr scampers behind me. In the lobby it is obvious there has been some kind of scene. You can feel it. The receptionist, Khek, is staring at the monitor in front of her – her face unusually flushed. She is close to tears. The bellman, Sith, is standing next to a trolley full of baggage, staring out the front doors as if contemplating an escape. The silence in the room is distinctly unnerving.

A short, rather tubby woman with greying, short hair and a grim squarish face is standing in front of the reception desk with her arms folded defiantly across her chest. She has a neck of loose mottled skin, shiny with perspiration. She's beyond middle-age and has given up concealing the decay. Now she stands with a sort of stubborn dignity; with unmistakeable purpose. It's that kind of formidable presence from which even death might cower. In a decidedly Thatcheresque twist, a shiny black leather handbag hangs awkwardly from her wrist.

'You must be the manager,' she says stiffly.

'The general manager,' I reply with a smile. I advance towards the computer behind the reception desk and peer at the screen. 'And I believe you must be ...'

'My name is Nancy Bacon.'

'Oh, yes, Mrs Bacon. I saw your name on the guest list this morning.' I pretend to have spotted her name on the screen. 'It seems as if we have some sort of trouble with your booking.'

'*Seems?*' she says. 'You've given me the *wrong room*. I specifically asked for the suite with a view of the stupa. A simple request you might think. But apparently not. For some reason, you've given me a suite with a view of some sort of office building. It's not what I asked for. I've prepaid for my stay and I expect you to deliver what I asked for.'

'Right. A view of the stupa.'

She's complaining about the view. I can't quite believe this is happening. I immediately think of Fawlty Towers – the episode with Mrs Richards. Remember that one? Mrs Richards was the old deaf battle-axe. She had a complaint about the view too. Basil, exasperated as usual, asked her what she might expect to see out of a Torquay hotel bedroom window. The Hanging Gardens of Babylon? The Sydney Opera House? No, she wanted a view of the sea and Basil pointed out that the sea was right there – between the land and the sky. But Mrs Richards was hardly satisfied. What was it he said? Might you move to a hotel closer to the sea or preferably in it? I loved that show. Terribly funny.

But this is no laughing matter.

I do what we all do. I look at the computer screen. I scroll this way and that. I click and double-click here and there, as if the computer will magically produce some kind of intelligent resolution to our predicament which, of course, it won't because even computers aren't that smart. But at least I look as if I'm doing something sensible.

'I'm afraid to say, Mrs Bacon, that it seems we've most certainly made a mess of things. I see that you expressly asked for the suite with a view of the stupa and that appears to have been allocated to another guest.'

'I've already been told that Mr ... Mr ...'

'Mr Lockhardt.'

'Mr Lockhardt. What I want to know is what you're going to do about it. I expect you to live up to your promises and give me the suite I asked for.'

'Well, Mrs Bacon we can't possibly do that.' I give her a smug little laugh.

'How dare you laugh!' she snaps. 'You're supposed to be the general manager! Now act like one, you oaf, and deliver my suite!'

Oaf? *Oaf?*

Now I can see why Farr and Khek and Sith are such blithering wrecks. I return to the screen.

'I'm afraid that's impossible, Mrs Bacon. The only suite we have with a view of the stupa is Room 604 and that, I'm afraid, is already occupied.'

The screen tells me that it's occupied by the British forestry company executive – an affable fellow; a regular. But this isn't the time to make any such admission.

I look up at her. 'I'm afraid it's occupied by the British Foreign Secretary.'

'Boris Johnson?'

'I errr,' I look back at the screen. That was a blunder. Way over the top. I could kick myself. 'I mean, I'm sorry, I meant Brunei. Yes, the Foreign Secretary of Brunei. Brunei, Britain, you know, easily confused.' I look up at her. I grip the mouse firmly, to stop my hand from shaking. 'He's a regular,' I add. 'A sultan.'

'And what's that supposed to mean? Who cares if he's a sultan?'

'Well, this could cause a most unfortunate international incident. You must see that we can't possibly turf the poor fellow out.'

'Well, I'm appalled,' she replies. She sighs deeply. Her pluck is abandoning her. I sense victory.

'The suite is available tomorrow and we'll certainly be able to move you to it at noon, as soon as the sultan departs. The sun will be up and you'll be able to enjoy the view of the stupa in all its glory.'

'I'm not here to *enjoy* the stupa, Mr Lockhardt.' She is tired and seems quite suddenly deflated. 'My flight was delayed in Bangkok. I've been shoved and shunted around airports for two days. I'm too tired now. I suppose I shall have to accept the room with the view of the office building.'

'I'm very grateful, madam.'

'While I'm still appalled.'

'I understand. I'm sorry.'

'I don't want your understanding or your apologies, Mr Lockhardt. I want you to keep your promises!'

'Yes, I'm afraid we're in a bit of pickle here.'

'Hmm,' she sniffs. 'You *smell* a bit pickled if you ask me.'

That hurts. It's true. I am pickled. I'm mostly pickled. I'm not proud of it. Fucking bitch.

I redden. And I see a hint of remorse in her narrow sharp-blue eyes. Remorse. I hope it hurts.

'Your suite tonight will be at no charge and please accept a complimentary cocktail in the Elephant Bar if you care to.'

'I don't drink, Mr Lockhardt.'

'Well, any kind of refreshment you like.'

'I'll take a cup of tea in my room.'

'Good idea. We'll have that sent up right away.'

I return to my room and crack open another can of beer. The TV half works. The left side of the screen is a greenish, pinkish whorl that squirms behind the glass like some sort of trapped alien. I picture it eventually bursting through the screen and throttling me. I laugh with relief. On the right side of the screen I see that the BBC is obsessing over BREXIT. I can't decide if I prefer that or the alien. There's a quarter bottle of vodka on the dresser. I open it and drink it slowly until it's finished, mesmerized by the alien behind the screen.

The following morning I am again at my desk. My ashtray is filling up nicely. Jacques is dithering around behind me, filing things in the filing cabinets. The steel drawers of the cabinets bang and crash as he opens and closes them.

'Could you keep it down?' I say. 'I'm trying to ... you know, work here.'

'Sorry,' Jacques says absently. He's not sorry. He hates me. He thinks I'm a fat loser.

I look back at the screen. Nancy Bacon is booked in for three months! Three! That's impossible! The bitch. No one stays at the Samarang for three months. The average booking, according to our records, is 1.75 days.

At best, we have those consultant types that stay for a month. The NGO crowd. They arrive and are chauffeur-driven to and from government ministries. They are experts in their field apparently and they spend their weekends at the poolside fixed on their laptops, cutting and pasting, tinkering with pie charts, bar graphs, poverty curves and all the metrics that postulate something they like to call an *international standard*. Then they go home again – a few grand the better for it, while their venerated report sits in some cupboard eaten alive by worms. This is what they call the 'liberal world order' hard at work.

But Nancy Bacon is not a consultant type. She's too prickly, too obstinate. She's not pretentious enough.

I see from the check-in documents that she holds a British passport. And yes, she did speak with a slightly plummy accent. But there was something else in the way she spoke that suggested Britain wasn't really hers. Some sort of brittle, metallic quality to her speech suggested Germanic or even Slavic origins. Then again, some of her words were oddly fluid, uttered with an almost gentle lilt. Woom instead of room. It could be a class thing, but it didn't seem like that. And even to look at her, I wouldn't say she was English. Yes, her eyes were distinctly blue, but the shape of them was almost Asian. And even though she was going grey, I could discern that her hair had once been jet black. The kind of hair that went with a naturally brownish skin. Southern Europe? North African? Middle Eastern? What a mysterious soul!

I obsess over these details. For some reason I am compelled to work out exactly who she is. I try to infer things from the data available to me and reach no useful conclusions. The last thing I'd do is ask her directly. I've already resolved that I would avoid her. Three months! If I spot her somewhere around the hotel I'll turn the other way, I'll pretend to be famously busy – occupied with sultans and foreign ministers. The bitch.

Jacques has finished his filing. 'Farr tells me there was a bit of a fiasco with a Mrs Bacon last night. She checked in late and her room had been taken.'

'Fiasco? The woman's a fucking viper. Be warned.'

'I see we're moving her to 604 today.'

'Yes, she wants a view of the stupa. I'll let you handle it.'

'Sure,' Jacques says with his usual misplaced confidence. He thinks he can handle her! Oh, how I'd love to be a fly on the wall!

'Ever had a strip torn off you by a woman called Bacon?'

I think this is enormously funny, but Jacques doesn't get it. Of course, he doesn't. He's French. Poor bastard.

I pop my head around the door of the Frangipani Room. It's almost full. The guests are enjoying their breakfast. The coffee smells good. The pastries are crispy and golden. They all seem to be engaged in convivial banter. I see the American couple and the

Korean delegation. I see the Irishman and the French family with two kids. I'm about to withdraw when I notice our British forestry executive sitting at the bay window. He's speaking to a woman who sits across the table from him. She has her back to me. It's her! Nancy Bacon! He's speaking with a bright smile and making elaborate gestures and she's laughing – genuinely laughing. He's such a jolly fellow. Simon is his name. A jolly fellow indeed. Everyone seems to like Simon. Even I like Simon. The prick.

I return to my office.

By 6 pm I have managed to avoid Nancy for the entire day. I have deliberately walked along the shaded corridors of the hotel with grim urgency, as if supremely busy, not to be delayed, just in case she sees me; wants to harangue me. But she hasn't seen me and I haven't seen her. I regard this as an important achievement.

The Russians are in the Fuchsia Room. It's their national day or something like that. I don't pop in. Russians scare me. They have an embassy over the hill. Built in the 70s out of giant slabs of concrete, it looks as if it was designed specifically for a bald man who whirs about in a wheelchair with a white fluffy cat sitting on his lap. There are rumours that it sits atop a labyrinthine network of subterranean tunnels.

I leave the hotel, skip down the front steps and walk briskly along the driveway lined with succulent shrubbery. It's not yet fully dark. Bats flit through the bluish murk. I'm almost at the front gate, about to veer into the street and bham, I bump into her; almost knock her down.

'Oh, God, Mrs Bacon! Are you all right? I almost knocked you down!'

She is a diminutive person. I'd given her a fright. She steadies herself. 'You seem to be in a hurry, Mr Lockhardt.'

'Oh yes. So I am. Need to dash downtown to ... you know ... attend to a few ... errands.'

'I see.' She looks up at me and studies me briefly. 'I met your sultan this morning.'

'My sultan?'

'Yes. It turns out his name is Simon and he's from Sussex.'

'A sultan from Sussex called Simon?'

'Yes,' she smirks. 'I thought it was odd too.'

I'm not in the mood to make anything up. Words fail me. So what if I'd lied? It worked didn't it?

'I suppose that's your tactic,' she adds. She sounds a bit weary.

'What do you mean?'

'You name drop. You drop names like little explosives. You use them like weapons.'

'That sounds a bit dramatic.'

'Hardly. Most of us do that.'

We stand in silence. A moped with a dim headlight rattles past.

'Right. Well. I hope you're comfortably settled into your suite. Enjoying the view of the stupa.'

'I've already told you that I'm not here to *enjoy* the stupa, Mr Lockhardt. But yes, I'm grateful to have a view of it. And yes, the suite is very comfortable, thank you.' She looks up at me and adds rather pointedly, 'That young French fellow was very helpful. Thank you.'

'Excellent. I'm very glad to hear it.'

She likes Jacques more than me. The bitch.

I hasten down the street, heading downtown; heading to the Destiny Pub. My favourite haunt. It has a strangely evocative name. But it's not a name I'd drop like a weapon – unless perhaps it was a weapon I'd use upon myself.

I see John Webb sitting at the counter. He's always sitting there, smoking cigarettes and drinking his French aperitif. 'Pastis!' he always says. 'It's cocaine-ish, that's why I drink it.' He calls himself an author. I even googled him once and couldn't find a single work he'd written. He likes me and I like him, even though he's a South African. He thinks he knows everything. Bumptious twat.

'John,' I say.

He stares at his glass of cocaine-ish fluid and says, 'Hello, Julian.'

I ask him about the Russians. Why are they so scary? Everyone is a bit scared of the Russians. This is a question that's bothered me for a long time.

John looks up at me and says, 'Well, it's obvious. They straddle the greatest clash of ideas known to mankind. Fatalism versus free will. They don't know what to make of it. They're confused. Confusion breeds anger and angry people are scary.'

I'm not sure I follow. I order a beer and look around the room. The girls are here. They're hanging around the pool tables, perched on bar stools, petite with powdered faces and painted fingernails. That's why I'm here. I'm not here to talk about the greatest clash of ideas known to mankind. Bumptious twat.

'See you,' I say and I march towards the pool tables. I love these girls. Asian girls. I can't tell if it's fatalism or free will. Who cares?

The girl I choose that night is one I've had before. I'd been hoping there might be a new one down at the Destiny Pub. They have a healthy staff turnover there. But Pon was there and she was friendly enough and even though I had my doubts (was still looking over my shoulder, scanning the room as we left, just in case there was a fresh face that I hadn't missed) I was moderately happy with my choice.

I unlock the steel gate at the back of the hotel and Pon and I skirt the pond, its moonlit lily pads, along a path fringed by fireflies, and head for the service entrance. Pon is not a talkative girl. That's probably why I chose her in the end. Nothing worse than sleeping with a chatterbox. Still, chatterbox or not, there is this thing with these girls that I can't quite fathom. Could it be more than just a transaction? Could it be the *real thing*? I am thrilled and mortified by the possibility. There are these little touches to this ritual that stun me. She showers. She folds the towel neatly across the towel rail. The towel mat is straightened alongside the shower stall. If she takes a pee, I almost expect to find the next sheet of toilet paper folded into a neat triangle. Why does she take all that trouble to keep things neat in my bathroom? It's never how I leave that room – awash with appalling odours and fluids, full of steam and sweat and the towels in a damp, soiled heap.

And whenever she takes the money she is so grateful, as if I've been unspeakably generous, I feel like bursting into tears. I'm not unspeakably generous. I pay the going rate. I know full well what the going rate is. I've been in this town long enough.

Pon leaves. My bathroom is sparkling, my cock limp, tingling and a little bit sore and it's as if she's never been in the room.

3

A Russian had been sick in one of the bathrooms adjoining the Fuchsia Room the night before.

Jacques tells me. I stare at him as he fusses over invoices on his desk. Such a French pretty boy (with a fucking huge nose and almost no top lip). He's so keen on his job. At a staff meeting I once asked him to say a few words. He implored the staff to believe in themselves; believe in the Samarang Hotel – the finest hotel in South East Asia.

Believe? What does that even mean? And I've been around long enough to know that the Samarang Hotel is just like any other. It's a business. It's a cruel, money-churning, profit-obsessed business that exists for one reason and one reason only: to make Mr Lim rich. How can Jacques ask them to believe in this place? It's as if he's trying to sell them some kind of religion.

The world isn't about belief. It's about numbers. Jacques doesn't get it.

Still, the Lao staff listen dutifully. Somehow they make me wonder if I don't get it either.

But let me tell you, I've been in this business a long time. Some people like to call it the 'hospitality game'. I don't. It's not a game. It's a business. And it's got nothing to do with hospitality.

I like hotels. I always have.

In 1971 – when I was 9 years-old – I got to stay in a hotel for the first time. My aunt, Shirley and her husband Trevor, were leaving the country, my old Rhodesia. Shirley was my mother's sister and my mother was unusually morose about it all. We travelled from Salisbury down to Umtali and then up into the Bunga Forest to stay at the Leopard Rock Hotel. My brother and I, we had our own room. It had a telephone. It had a TV. Crisp white sheets. A control panel next to the bed by which we could tune the radio, dim the lights and set the alarm. It had little cakes of soap wrapped in delicate paper embossed with the hotel crest. Brand new slippers and dressing gowns in the closet. It even had a minibar with tiny bottles of Scotch in a tiny fridge. The whole thing was titillating.

And do you know that Queen Elizabeth II and her mother stayed there in 1953? My mother had reminded us of this illustrious fact at every opportunity. This wasn't just any hotel. It was the best! The best in the country!

My brother, Daniel, who was much older than me, was so enthralled by the idea of us having our own room, one so luxuriously appointed, he even grew a boner on our first night. I grew a boner too. Lying on our beds, we shrieked with laughter. He tugged at his with vigour, finally yielding a spectacular, if unsightly result. I tugged at mine too, taken by the idea of it, even if I fell asleep trying to do what he had done.

In all other respects, it was, as far as I can recall, an utterly insufferable weekend. My parents spent all their time with Shirley and Trevor, arguing under an umbrella on the front lawn, beseeching them to stay, imploring them to note the violent beauty of the Bunga Forest. But for Shirley and Trevor, their tickets were booked. Their household packed. They were on their way to London and they prevailed helplessly on my parents to do the same.

Still, it was the hotel that I remember. It was the idea that there was a place – *just one small place* – on planet earth where people would take care of you. I resolved (I'm sure I did) that one day I'd work, I'd put on my distinguished, embossed uniform and work at a beautiful hotel, just like the Leopard Rock. I'd take care of people when they're away from home.

As it happens, I never got the chance to work at the Leopard Rock. In 1975, there was a coup in Portugal (Portugal! Of all places!) and the eastern border of Rhodesia was assailed by communist-inspired, liberation-minded, revolutionary heroes who now had refuge in Mozambique – Portugal's old colony.

They killed my brother, those heroes. They planted a Soviet-made landmine on a sandy road just outside Umtali. Blew him to bits. He was a soldier. Died for his country.

But that was all a long time ago.

Now Nancy Bacon accosts me in the corridor. She literally accosts me. She steps out from behind a Chinese fan palm in the corridor and stops me in mid-stride. It's an ambush!

'I'm not one to complain Mr Lockhardt,' she says (plaintively).

'Really?'

'But I do think you should have a word with the doorman.' I look up beyond the lobby and I see Sith. He's watching us. He's scowling. I've never seen him do that before.

'Sith? Sith the doorman?'

'I don't know what his name is, but yes, the doorman. At first I thought it was just a coincidence but every time I go anywhere near the front doors of the hotel, he refuses to stand up and open them. He does it for all the other guests, with some alacrity I might add, but never does it for me. He's always suddenly magically busy. And now, I've just walked up the front steps and he sat on his little stool, watching me. He simply refused to move. I had to tug at those huge doors myself and he simply sat and stared at me. It's not the way a doorman should behave.'

'It most certainly isn't. I'll look into it.'

I talk to Sith. He's about my age and has been a doorman at this hotel since he was a youngster. 'She should go home,' he says sullenly.

'Why do you say that?'

'She impolite.'

'But Sith, we have lots of impolite people stay here. Lots!'

'Yes, but she should go home.'

Sith is obstinate. It's as if it should be obvious – not worthy of an explanation.

'Sith. What is it? What has she done?'

After a long pause, with Sith looking at the floor filled with anguish and quite possibly murderous intent, he says, 'I've been doorman here for long time. I am happy to be doorman. Everyone friendly. But this lady ... this lady, when she walk to the door she is staring at me and then she stop and she wait. She stare at me and wait. I don't like it.'

I can picture it.

'I don't like it either, Sith,' I say. 'But remember we've been through this before. This is a hotel. And we just have to do whatever they want. Remember? The customer is always right?'

Sith visibly reddens when I tell him that. He doesn't like it. He wants to explode.

People come to this country and like to complain about poor service. Sometimes, when you walk into a restaurant the staff are all sitting at the back chatting. They see you enter, but they just sit and chat as if you – the customer – are the least important thing in the world. They're waiting for you to go over and ask them for a menu. You have to *ask* for the menu. And when they deliver the food they just deliver whatever comes out of the kitchen first. There's no co-ordination. It's quite possible that your lunching companion will have finished his lunch before yours has even arrived! Poor service. People like to complain.

But somehow I think it's unfair.

John Webb had once said: 'If they don't fawn over you just because you've got a fistful of notes in your pocket, isn't there something dignified, something honourable in that?'

I think I know what he means. We're constantly assailing each other with sales pitches. But not here. And it's more of a relief than an annoyance.

But still, we do staff training. We point out that the Samarang Hotel is the leading hotel in the country and that – at least in the precincts of the hotel grounds – the customer gets what the customer wants. This is when Jacques gets almost weepy with his exhortations that we regard this venerated establishment as some sort of religious experience. Still, we have a high staff turnover. These locals – they just don't buy it. They don't buy the supreme power of the customer. It almost offends them.

Sith is our longest serving staff member. He is the friendliest person at the hotel. He might even be the friendliest person in all of Asia. I like him and I'd be devastated if he left. But here, after many decades of loyal service it seems as if he's ready to flee. All because of Nancy-bloody-Bacon.

'I'll talk to her, Sith. Don't worry.'

After lunch I spot Nancy. She's trudging down the corridor towards the pool. She wears a white sarong with giant blue and yellow flowers printed on it and she carries a bag full of books.

'Oh, Mrs Bacon, I'm glad I caught you.'

She turns and glares at me in her usual fierce manner.

'If you have a minute.'

'I'm on my way to the pool.' She turns and continues on her way. 'But yes, I have a minute.'

So, now I follow her, jabbering like some forlorn servant, while she glides towards the gardens with her sarong flowing out behind her.

'I just wanted to talk to you about the doorman.'

'Oh yes?'

'Yes, well the thing is, you know … this is a Buddhist country and the thing is …'

She stops. She turns. She has a cruel smirk on her face. 'I'm quite aware that this is a Buddhist country, Mr Lockhardt.'

'Yes, of course you are. And the thing is, you know, they can be a bit sensitive. I mean, losing face … that sort of thing.'

She gives me a rather scathing laugh. 'Losing face? You really don't have the faintest idea what you're talking about, do you,

Mr Lockhardt?'

'I ... I ... well.'

No, I didn't have the faintest idea. I know nothing about these people – these Buddhists – and how they lose face. All I really know is that they might be softly-spoken, but they don't like to be dicked around. That's the extent of my cultural sensitivity. I'm just trying to stand up for Sith – the doorman who refuses to open the door.

'Well the thing is that he's a very good and loyal member of our staff and I suppose he feels a bit intimidated by you and, you know... we are all people after all.'

Nancy looks out at the gardens thoughtfully. 'I've stayed at this hotel before, Mr Lockhardt. Before your time. It used to be run by a lovely man. Bill, if I recall correctly.'

'Ah, yes. Bill Carstens. My predecessor. Yes, he was ... very well liked, I'm sure. Very sad when he popped off. A great loss to the Samarang.'

As I speak I detect that familiar weariness in her face. It seems to move over her like a shadow. She looks up at me. She has more words. I can tell. But she seems too tired to even try. Finally, she says, 'Well, thank you for telling me about the doorman. It's not really my business to go around intimidating people.'

'I'm very grateful.'

It's true. I am very grateful. She'd been surprisingly forgiving of poor Sith and even though she'd alluded to my predecessor, suggesting that he did a better job than me (the bitch), I feel enormously relieved that the controversy over the doorman has been properly resolved.

I am pleased with myself and almost feel like skipping down the corridor back to my office – even humming a little tune. As I walk away, she calls out to me. 'Mr Lockhardt?'

I turn.

'How long have you lived in this country?'

'Six years,' I reply.

'I see. Well I suppose some of it has rubbed off on you. We are all people, as you say. It's an odd thing for a hotel manager to say.'

I gulp and blush and feel somewhat unsure about myself. 'Yes. Yes, I suppose it is.'

I return to my office. Why had she mentioned Bill Carstens? I fume whenever I hear his name. He was a whoring old drunk. No one liked Bill Carstens. I've never heard a good thing said about him. The Samarang was plummeting into little more than a damp third-rate borstal under his stewardship. No one liked him. Whenever I think of him I feel a kind of anger rising up inside me. No one compares me to Bill-fucking-Carstens – bless his soul.

Jacques springs into the room. He's in a state. This is unusual.

'The Russian!' he cries. 'The one in 515.'

'Yes?'

'He's dead in the bath!'

I feel this terrible prickliness run through my body – from my head to my toes.

'Dead in the bath?'

'Yes. Housekeeping took a look inside. He'd had the Do-Not-Disturb tag on the door the whole day and all of last night. They became suspicious. He's dead in the bath.'

'Oh fuck.'

The night before, the hotel was brimming with heavy-drinking Russians, and now one of them is dead in the bath. I watch enough cable news to know how this looks.

I call Mr Lim.

He is untroubled by the news. That's the problem with Mr Lim. He's always untroubled. He tells me that we should phone the police. It seems as if he is inclined to wash his hands of the whole affair. The management of the hotel – including dead Russians – is my business. Profits are his.

'But he's *Russian*!' I say querulously.

'So?'

'Well a dead Russian is far more problematic. I mean I'd hardly be concerned if he was from New Zealand or, you know, somewhere *nice*.'

'I don't know what you mean,' he says.

I ask Khek to call the police. By now the word has already spread throughout the hotel. There's a dead Russian on the fifth floor.

I sit in my office and smoke.

I don't want to inspect the room. I don't want to see the bluish, naked body of an asphyxiated Russian in the bath. Why would I? And it occurs to me that the room may well be a crime scene. I'd rather have nothing to do with it.

But Jacques is aghast. 'You're the general manager! You can't just leave this up to Souk and Seng!'

Souk and Seng are the two members of the housekeeping staff who discovered the body.

And with acid sarcasm, he adds, 'The *apex* of power?'

He turns on his heel and sashays out of the office.

So I go up to Room 515. Dead bodies aren't my thing. Souk and Seng are standing at the end of the corridor next to their cleaning trolley. They are decidedly subdued.

I bound towards them. 'Good morning, ladies.'

They nod warily.

'I'm sorry about all this. Hope you're all right. Awful thing.'

Their English isn't too good.

'I mean. Very bad. I very sorry. You okay?'

They nod again.

'The police come soon.'

They are hardly mollified. I look up at the door of Room 515. He's right there, on the other side of this piece of wood. I'm trying to think of a reason to delay this, but Souk and Seng stare at me expectantly.

Do you know that I'm fifty-six and I've never seen a dead body? Isn't that amazing? Think of it. Think of the millions – billions! – of people who have died all around me over the last fifty-six years and not once have I seen a dead body. I mean, not up close. I've seen my fair share on the sides of roads after car accidents. They looked pretty much dead to me as I drove past, slightly captivated. But this is the first time that I get to see one and hang around, inspect it for as long as I care to.

I'm prevaricating, I know. I take one more glance at Souk and Seng, offer them a faltering smile, slide my master key into the electronic slot and enter Room 515. Aside from the bedclothes that are dishevelled and twisted and hanging over the side of the bed, the room looks oddly normal. The first thing that strikes me is that the man might not be dead at all. This is something I've often thought about. How do we know when a body actually dies? The Americans debate endlessly over when life begins, but I've never heard much about when life ends. What are the empirical facts we use to determine that?

I walk with unexpected calmness to the bathroom. I see his arm first. It's hanging over the edge of the bath. Yes, he's dead. I can tell just by looking at the arm. It's stiffened and rubbery and a distinctly blue-grey. His head is to one side, resting against the tiles. Mouth agape. Eyes shut. The water in the bath is a murky grey. His pectoral muscles sag with forlorn resignation and his hairy belly seems oddly bloated as if it might suddenly pop.

There is water on the floor. The towel mat is drenched. There is a drip from the tap. I consider leaning forward and tightening it and then I think the better of it. Fingerprints. Dead Russians. Avoid it.

I glance at the adjoining shower stall and note thick wiry hair congregated around the plughole.

I step back. On the dresser I see a foil tab of pills. Enalapril maleate. Blood pressure drugs. I know this because I take them myself. There's a laptop next to the bed. There's a USB stick inserted into the side. I'm thinking of blueprints of nuclear plants, formulae for lethal nerve agents, videos of a naked Donald Trump being pissed on by a glamorous whore.

I want to leave. Why? I have this very odd feeling that, somehow, the man is not dead. He's still around. I walk with considerable stealth towards the door as if he might suddenly yell to me from the bathroom, complain of my intrusion while he's taking his bath!

At the door, I stop. The closet is slightly ajar. It's tantalizing. I can't help myself.

I steal my way to the closet and using the back of my hand I draw the closet door open. The safe! Of course! I'm suddenly plunged into a state of giddying speculation. The safe will need to be opened. Could I trust the local police with the contents? And what of the Russians? You can hardly trust the Russians. I suddenly feel compelled to open the safe. Justice! Truth! Cover ups! These words are roaring in my head. I place my hand on the closet door to steady myself. I have the master codes in my pocket. I could open it right now. I could defend the free world!

But then I hear something of a commotion outside. A car comes to a stop in the driveway with a screech of its tyres. I run to the window and peep through a gap in the curtain. A shiny black SUV with diplomatic plates has arrived. Four men in suits jump out. The Russian are coming!

I walk briskly to the door, take one final glance at the room and leave.

Souk and Seng are still standing in the corridor. It seems that they're disinclined to do any more housekeeping today. Poor frazzled creatures.

'Why don't you go home? Take the rest of the day off. It's okay.'

This they understand and they set about pushing their trolley to the service elevator. I walk the other way, to the guest elevators.

When the elevator doors open I am confronted by the four Russians. I know they're Russian. Their neckties are loose around their necks, as if they're a nuisance; a contrivance from the Western world that they feel compelled to wear if they want to be taken seriously.

They walk towards me and the tall one says, 'Mr Lockhardt. We're from the embassy. The Russian embassy. Consular Affairs. We're here about Mr Andropov, a Russian citizen. He is dead yes? In Room 515?'

'I ... he ... yes, he's dead. I'm ... we've called the local police. They should be here any minute now.'

'Never mind about the local police, Mr Lockhardt. He's a Russian citizen. It's a matter for the Russian state.'

I can't quite believe this is happening. And how the hell do they know my name? I can't say I've ever seen any of these men before.

'Right. Well, I do think we should wait for the local police. I mean, you know, this isn't actually ... Russia. It's a ... you know, sovereign state.'

The tall man has already started down the corridor, expecting me to follow him. He turns on me and says, 'Come, Mr Lockhardt. Open the door. You have the key, yes?'

The three other men stand close to me, in my way of the elevators. One of them smells distinctly of sausages. They offer me few alternatives.

I am suddenly struck by an image of Nancy. Yes, Nancy Bacon! I picture her standing at the reception desk, bristling over the view from her room and I feel oddly inspired.

'I have the key. Of course I do.' I push my way through the three men who crowd around me and press the elevator button. 'I am the general manager of the Samarang Hotel and now, if you'll all follow me we will wait in the lobby until the police arrive'. The elevator gives a ping with meticulous timing and I put my arm out ushering them all into the car.

This is followed by the most appalling silence. I realise that the elevator doors will soon close and my theatrical display of defiance will suddenly fade into an utter folly.

But the tall man instructs two of his henchmen to stand at the door to Room 515 while he and his remaining colleague step into the elevator.

'*All* of you please. I'm not having your people loafing about the corridors,' I say primly.

The tall one smiles at me in a way that is slightly threatening, slightly indignant. I can't tell which is worse. He orders his remaining colleagues into the elevator.

The doors close. Encapsulated in that small space the Russians and I wait in silence until the tall one says, 'I think you need to press the button for the ground floor.'

'Oh. Yes. I suppose I do.'

I put the Russians in the Elephant Bar and offer them coffee, compliments of the hotel. 'Do let me know if there's anything more we can do to make your stay more comfortable,' I say.

They look at me with evident resentment.

I'd always assumed that the police in this country were stricken by a remarkable lack of curiosity. But they arrive promptly. First, two uniformed officers arrive on a moped. And hot on their heels, some slightly more decorated officers – as far as I can tell from their epaulettes – arrive in a brand-new sedan.

Jacques and I sit in the office. We're both feeling uneasy. He's disturbed by the death of the Russian, as am I. But he's also annoyed with *me*; my unwillingness to relieve Souk and Seng of their grim discovery. Neither of us talk. We pretend to engage in various administrative tasks.

It's not long before the tall Russian and his sausage-smelling cohort walk in. They don't knock. They just walk in and stand in front of my desk, staring at me.

'The CCTV footage. You must give us the footage. We must make an investigation.'

I lean back in my chair and sigh stiffly. 'I'll need to hear that from the police, Mr … Mr …'

But he does not divulge his name. He mutters something to the sausage man who scuttles out of the room. 'You take pride in this hotel, Mr Lockhardt,' he says.

'I suppose I do. Now, would you mind waiting in the Elephant Bar? This is a private office.'

He ignores me, leaning casually against a filing cabinet. 'This is a very serious matter. I'm getting the feeling you are not seeing that. This is a shame, yes?'

This is a distinctly threatening remark. Sweat suddenly seems to spring from my armpits. I shrug sulkily and return to the papers on my desk.

'Mr Andropov died in this hotel. You should pray that there is nothing suspicious about it. Mr Andropov was a friend of the Russian government. Your co-operation would be wise.'

'I'm sure it would. Now, I'd like to get back to work, if you don't mind. I'm quite sure there is nothing suspicious about it.

People die in hotel rooms all the time. Even Russians.'

The Russian gives me a sly smile.

'He was in good health,' he says, speaking of Mr Andropov. 'A little younger than you. A little slimmer too. He didn't smoke and didn't drink. At least it seems unusual that such a man would die in his bath.'

I recall the dead man's blood pressure tablets on the dresser. I recall how the bedclothes were in a state of disarray. Sign of a struggle? And why was there a wiry knot of hair in the plughole of the shower stall? Did he prefer a shower to a bath? And if so, why was the bath his final resting place?

Despite these suspicions, I say nothing.

The sausage man returns. He is followed by a local policeman. The Russians and the policeman have an urgent conversation in the local language. Jacques and I glance at each other in a rare moment of solidarity, drawn together by our pitiful command of the Lao language. The policeman, a delicate Asian man in an oversized uniform, looks at me from across the room and says, 'The CCTV. You must give.' He betrays all emotion. He speaks in a monotone.

'Right. Of course.'

Jacques, in charge of day-to-day security arrangements, stands and walks to a desk in the corner of the room. 'Here,' he says, 'is the system. The feed erases itself every 48 hours.' He moves towards the monitor and reaches for the mouse.

The Russians push him aside.

'This is the hard drive?' says one, pointing at the processor under the desk.

Jacques nods.

The two Russians lean down and pull the processor away from the wall. They unplug the cables, lift the machine up and carry it out of the room without another word, and the policeman follows them.

'Fuck,' I say after a long pause. 'We should have got ourselves a copy.'

I bury my head in my hands.

Jacques issues a lofty little laugh. I look up at him. He is smiling; seems pleased with himself. He opens a drawer of his desk and produces a flash drive. 'I did already.'

I suddenly think that I might end up liking that pompous little prick.

In the afternoon Mr Lim arrives in his enormous black Lexus. He is a tiny man in his eighties with little more than a wisp of white hair on his speckled head. He totters into the hotel, blinks and walks towards me, smiling broadly.

'Hello, Mr Juwy,' he says. That's what he calls me. I've stopped trying to correct him.

'Mr Lim, I'm glad to see you.'

He dips his head slightly, still smiling. 'The man he dead. He okay?'

It's a strange way to frame the question, but I know what he means. 'Yes. He's okay. Everything is okay. He's, you know, dead.'

'Ah good, very good. The police they come?'

'Yes, yes. The police have been. And the Russian embassy. So, they're dealing with it. Everything is fine. Absolutely fine. Completely under control.'

'Ah good, very good.' He looks around the lobby. Sith, the doorman, and Khek, the receptionist, smile at him. He smiles back at them. He takes me with surprising firmness by the arm and we begin to walk towards the corridor that leads to the pool. 'So, Mr Juwy, we do ceremony. Okay? You tell Khek to do. She know all. She know how to do. We do ceremony for the man he die.'

'Yes, a ceremony. That's a very good idea.'

He stops and looks up at me. He is a very old man and I'm suddenly stirred by a rare jolt of affection for him. 'You okay, Mr Juwy?'

'I ... ummm, yes, thank you. Fine. Completely fine.'

He smiles at me broadly and gives me a fatherly pat on the back. 'Okay, very good. It okay. The guy he dead. It okay.'

I suddenly want Mr Lim to stay. I'd never wanted that. I liked the way he gave me a pat on the back. He's never done that in all the six years that I've known him. But he shuffles off, through the front doors, climbs into his Lexus and drives away.

I'm in serious need of a drink and it's well before sundown when I reach the Destiny Pub.

John Webb is in his usual place. 'I hear you got yourselves a dead Russian,' he says while staring at the shiny surface of his milky drink.

'Fuck me if the news doesn't travel fast in this town,'

'Either way, I'd rather not,' he grunts.

I sit down next to him and order a beer.

'The thing is,' I say. 'How do we know when we're actually dead? I mean, we all make a huge fuss about when we're born

– you know, the Americans and the way they carry on about abortion, but how do we know when we're *dead*?'

John Webb is silent for some time and then he says, 'I've no fucking idea. If they put you in a box and you're unable to move and they close the lid, who's to say? You're stuck there while your hair and your fingernails keep on growing.'

'Well that's the scariest thing I've ever thought of.'

John Webb downs his drink and orders another.

I continue, 'I suppose the only real saving grace is that, either way, you won't have long to go. In that box. In the grand scheme of things. Just grin and bear it, until they set it on fire and make sure.'

'Not long,' John confirms. 'Unless there's some kind of ridiculous delay. A mortuary worker's strike. A power failure at the crematorium. The environmental lobby get going with some campaign that halts the burning of corpses because of the greenhouse emissions. Protests in the streets. Bodies in boxes piling up. It'd be on all the news networks. Could be stuck there for weeks. Months! Without a smoke!'

We look up from our drinks and face each other, both stricken by the horror of it.

4

The point is that the Russians *are* the bad guys.

Everybody knows this.

And the Americans are the good guys. Well, the WMD debacle put that in some doubt. And the financial crash. And *Yes We Can* turned out to be *Maybe We Can't*. And Trump is as thick as a plank. But still, Americans are the good guys. That hasn't really changed. It can't be easy being the world's only superpower. Frankly, if there is to be only one superpower, I'm glad it's not the Russians. And I'm glad it's not the Chinese. There's something about that Cultural Revolution that unsettles me. They carry on as if it never really happened. They still put huge posters of him, conspicuously in every public square. Wasn't he supposed to be a tyrant? How can they be so blasé about it, so forgiving of tyranny? Perhaps I don't understand it, but it really unsettles me.

The Americans invented rock 'n roll! And the hamburger and soft-serve ice-cream and the drive-thru! They invented cars with cup holders! They created the sitcom and the blockbuster! Fine, that may not be the same as the jet engine or the computer, but they've invented a lot of fun stuff. What other nation can claim to live in pursuit of happiness quite as keenly as America? And that's what we're all after, right? Happiness?

What was Russia's moment of innovative genius? The AK-47?

And the Europeans are a sour lot. Depressing operas, the Swiss Army knife and the Hadron Collider. They're not in pursuit of happiness. They're in pursuit of *existence*. These are very different things.

John Webb – the old soak – tells me that the Russians are confused. They're stuck in the middle of the greatest clash of ideas known to mankind. So now they're angry. But I get the feeling that we're all angry. Perhaps we're just better at concealing it with our famously smug pretensions and utterly delusional optimism.

I'll tell you one thing though: John doesn't like the idea of dying; doesn't like the idea of being stuck in a box, unable to move and being burned at over a thousand degrees.

That much we agree on. No confusion there.

The following morning Jacques and I don't do a stitch of work. We are transfixed by the footage. We stare for hours at the image of the fifth-floor corridor. I've never experienced such compulsive viewing. We see our Russian guest check in. We see the bellman arrive with his luggage. We see the bellman leave. His shoulders droop distinctively. No tip, probably. Russians aren't known for their largesse. We see the Russian leave in the evening. We follow him, switching to the elevator cameras, and the lobby cameras and the hallway cameras that lead to the Fuchsia Room. He was an attendee at the Russian party. It's impossible to see what he drinks. Could be water, could be soda, could be vodka. The embassy man had told me that Mr Andropov did not drink. So, apparently, it's not vodka. We follow him to the bathroom, down the corridor from the Fuchsia Room. He is in there for seventeen minutes and thirty-six seconds!

'He must have been the one who was sick!' Jacques exclaims.

This is a potentially significant finding. Again, Jacques impresses me.

'Exactly!' I say as if I'd reached precisely the same conclusion.

Mr Andropov leaves the party early. He doesn't appear to be out of sorts. He's just as glum and dispirited as he was when he arrived. We follow him back to his room. He closes the door. Minutes later, he opens the door and places the Do-Not-Disturb tag on the doorknob. And that is the last we see of Mr Andropov.

Remaining footage shows Souk and Seng arrive the following morning. They shuffle past his room, observing the instructions that hang from the doorknob. By 14:00, according to policy, they knock. Nothing. They return at 14:22. They knock. Still nothing. They knock again. After a few minutes, Souk opens the door. She enters the room. A few seconds later, she is back. Something is clearly awry. They speak to each other with unusual urgency and appear to be a bit jittery. They return to the room together. After a few seconds they are back in the corridor. They leave their cleaning trolley at the door and hurry down towards the service elevator.

Thirty-five minutes later I arrive. I am captivated by my image as I lope down the corridor, weighed down with trepidation. I am in that room for all of three minutes.

When I leave I talk briefly to Souk and Seng and then head down the corridor.

Jacques clicks the 'stop' icon and the video image is frozen.

It's just me, a dark grey smudge at the end of the corridor, about to spring for the alcove that houses the guest elevators. A ghost-like figure.

'That's it?'

'That's it,' Jacques confirms.

'So,' I say, 'Andropov must have been the sick one. The one who threw up all over the bathroom floor.'

'It's been cleaned,' Jacques says. 'Impossible to check for samples.'

Jacques is surprisingly astute.

'Right. Well, at least he didn't eat any of the food at the party, as far as we can tell. They can't accuse us of food poisoning.'

There is nothing more to make of it.

Khek enters the office. She bows deferentially at the two of us as we sit on our swivel chairs and stare back at her. She is here in the nerve centre of the hotel operations – the situation room, if you like. A little deference seems appropriate.

'Khek,' I say. 'What's up?'

Khek requests funds for the ceremony. 'We invite nine monks to do ceremony. We have to give something for them and for the Elder. Some food and other thing for the temple.'

I refer her to Jacques. He produces one hundred dollars from petty cash. Khek is grateful. She bows and leaves the room.

'A hundred bucks!' I say. 'Seems a bit cheap.'

Khek returns half an hour later. 'We do ceremony at three o' clock. Nine monk, they come. You and Mr Jacques come. We do blessing in room. Mr Lim come too. Okay?'

I have never been to a Buddhist ceremony before. Religious

ceremonies aren't my thing. Religion isn't my thing. I'm almost comforted by the prospect that religion is gradually becoming defunct. The Muslims might still be titillated by it, but they'll come around.

I've been invited to Buddhist ceremonies before, but never accepted. True, I've been to local weddings – vast affairs which involve a bit of dancing and plenty of Johnnie Walker – but that's as close to a ceremony as I've come to in this little place.

Khek leaves and I review the guest list for today. The sultan called Simon from Sussex is checking out. Two American business travellers are checking in. My mother had a dim view of Americans. 'Spend 30 seconds with an American and they'll know everything about you.' Quizzy, is how she described them. I suppose that's right. Other new arrivals include an Italian, an Argentinian and three Chinese. An Australian couple with two children have taken the suite and a neighbouring room on the sixth floor. And there's a Swede, a Singaporean, a Latvian and three Turks. Nothing we can't handle. I'm grateful there are no more Russians on the list.

And as for the events we have the Canadians hosting a Trade Facilitation Working Group Meeting in the Bougainvillea Room. This will need to be cleared out at 15:00 sharp, to make preparations for the Indonesian Investment Summit opening cocktail party. The Fuchsia Room is booked by the Dutch Embassy which is hosting an event to welcome three Dutch parliamentarians who are involved in a gender equality research project. A Hong Kong law firm is hosting a lunch in the Orchid Room.

I leave the office and the two American travellers have just arrived. They are walking towards the reception desk – two tall, cleanly shaven, well-built, smartly dressed men with confident smiles. They're almost impossibly healthy with an unashamedly positive outlook on life. One looks like Ben Affleck and the other looks like a youngish Harrison Ford. I know immediately what this is. They are either members of the Church of Jesus Christ of Latter Day Saints or The Seventh Day Adventists or maybe even the Living Waters Episcopalian Ministries. You can spot them a mile off. There is a surprising number of these types of Americans who visit this part of the world

I peer into the Elephant Bar. There is a group of distinctively Middle Eastern-looking men, wearing dark glasses, sitting in a group drinking coffee. In the Frangipani Room, two Frenchmen are muttering to each other while they nibble surreptitiously on pastries. There's an Englishman sitting fully-clothed by the pool, pretending to read a newspaper. He reveals himself by peeping over the top of the paper every few seconds, as if monitoring a wondrously immobile Indian sprawled on a lounger under an umbrella.

Given recent events, I have a slightly queasy feeling that the hotel is riddled with spies. Riddled!

I feel sweat break out on my forehead and a strange urge to run; to run away from this place, far away to nowhere. I want nowhere. No man's land.

In the afternoon nine bald-headed Buddhist monks in their bright orange robes sit in a cross-legged row along the wall. I, in my venerated position as the general manager, sit in a prominent position, right before them. On either side of me sit Mr Lim and

Khek. Other staff members are there too. Jacques and Sith, Souk and Seng, some of the kitchen staff, some of the waiters, one of the hotel drivers. We're all in Room 515. The furniture has been pushed against the walls so that there is adequate space for the ceremony. The windows are open. Birds twitter in the tree outside.

The senior monk is a very old and frail fellow. They stare ahead as if none of us are in the room.

And then the ceremony begins. It's the chanting. I've heard it before – from a distance, never up close. Now I am on my knees. I take my lead from Mr Lim. I bow. I press my palms together in prayer. And it doesn't take long before I am seized by the fluidity, the ceaseless motion of the voices. I am struck – entirely absorbed – by an image of a river. It has a glinting surface, it curls and slips around the smooth, unmoving rocks on its banks. It gurgles through the reeds. It flexes and gleams in the sunlight and I am carried along with it, held by the rhythm of the chant, the rhythm of the water, the rhythm of my beating heart. I am helplessly free, swept along, and helplessly trapped, swirling in its grip. I yield entirely to this thing – this … this image – and I want to cry with the joy of it; the horror of it.

It seems as if I am there for a long time. With a sort of mechanical sluggishness, I mimic the gestures that Mr Lim performs by my side. Bowing occasionally and pressing my palms against the floor. Straightening up and facing the nine monks. The senior monk dips a bushel of green leaves into a silver bowl and shakes it outwards at the people who kneel before him. I feel the scented droplets, cool and clear, on my face. The chanting continues.

The group of people behind me – the ones who speak the local language – occasionally offer a unified lament, in response to which the monks resume with their chant. And still the river stays with me. Eyes open, eyes shut. It's doesn't matter. It stays with me. I am by its side. I am in it. I *am* it.

When the ceremony ends, I continue to kneel. The monks are rising to leave. Ordinarily, as dignified guests, I'd stand with my usual fawning charm, shake all their hands and thank them for coming. But I remain fixed to the floor. Me and my river. I feel the image curling away from me, slowly shrouded in a growing mist. I raise my hands to my face. It is wet. I can't be sure if these are tears. I roll over onto my rear and look behind me. The group is departing. As they move towards the door, I spot one other person who kneels near the wardrobe. It's Nancy Bacon. I watch her vaguely, not sure what to make of her presence at the back of the room.

I stand with a groan. I face her and she faces me. I don't want to talk to her. I don't want to talk at all. To anyone. She nods with a shy smile.

I leave Room 515 and use the service elevator to the ground floor. I walk swiftly along the corridor, assiduously ignoring everyone; their appalling babble, their insufferable pretensions and bleating neediness. I hear them all around me, going this way and that. They all seem vaguely hysterical. I quicken my pace, return to my room, close the door, lie face down on my bed and sob into the pillow with hopeless abandon.

I cry for so long that I begin to wonder if I might ever be able to stop. I picture myself staggering about for what is left of my turn on this petty little planet, my head drooping, constantly reddish, constantly leaking, suffused with inexplicable shame. I'll never again be able to lift my sodden face to the rest of the human race.

I do finally regain some sort of composure. I shower, feel the water on my body, hear it splashing against the glass and gurgling down the hole. I begin to dress. I'm supposed to pop in to the Dutch Ambassador's party – the one for the parliamentarians who are interested in gender equality. I think of the ambassador. Wouter is his name. He's a witty, urbane, well-educated man. You know what they say about the Dutch, right? They're Germans who think they're English. Wouter likes me. We always share a joke or two at these things.

But no. Not tonight. I remove my crisp white shirt and formal black trousers. I put on a T-shirt and jeans and sneakers and I leave the hotel with glum, mindless urgency. I can't handle the Dutch. Just not right now.

At the gate I encounter Nancy. It's almost in exactly the same spot where I last bumped into her and at exactly the same time of day. That time, she'd accused me of using names like weapons.

'Mr Lockhardt, in a hurry again?'

'I … yes. So I am. Hello, Mrs Bacon.'

'Oh you might as well call me Nancy.' She laughs drily.

'Julian,' I say and then I put out my hand. I don't know why I do this. We've already met; already know each other. What on earth are we doing shaking hands?

She takes my hand and looks up at me with a slightly intense curiosity. 'You don't like your name, do you?'

'My name? Julian?'

She nods, still smiling.

'Well, it's all right.' I feel myself reddening. 'I mean, it's not one I would have chosen, but here it is. Had it for fifty-six years and still going strong.'

This is followed by a long pause.

'Well,' she says, looking down at the paving stones, 'I've never really liked mine. Nancy. Nancy Bacon. It's hardly seductive. It's no Sofia or Tiffany or something like that. It's ... it's a frumpish sort of name. I wonder how much it has defined me.'

'Well, I'm sure that can't be true. Nancy is charming. It's ... you know ... charming.'

She gives another of those dry, slightly dismissive laughs.

'You were at the ceremony today,' I said. 'Caught me a bit by surprise. I thought it was only for the staff. You know these Buddhists they tend to get a bit skittish over this kind of thing.'

'What *kind of thing*?'

I can feel her familiar steeliness re-emerging. It's obvious she doesn't approve of my remark.

'Well ... spirits and whatnot.'

'Hmmm,' she muses, returning to face the paving stones. 'It seemed to me that you might have been quite moved by the ceremony. Were you?'

'I ... I ...' I'm stunned by the question. I feel seized, yet again, by that appalling shakiness. 'I was. Yes. I was moved. That's exactly what I felt.'

We head our separate ways. I consider the word, 'moved'. I've heard of people being 'moved' – emotionally or spiritually or whatever it is. But it strikes me that for the first time this is precisely what I feel. I even recall a glimpse of that mighty moving river.

I see John Webb in his usual place. 'How's it going with the dead Russian?' he says. He seems amused by the incident; as if it is my deserved lot.

'We had a ceremony today. The monks came. Did a lot of chanting.'

'Ah!' he says. 'I like those.'

'Ceremonies?'

'Yes,' he turns on his barstool to face me. 'I like ceremonies. They bring people together. That's harder to do than it seems. And they're designed to make us think. Think a little bit about what our lives are.'

I order a beer and I decide to tell him about the image I had of the river. I don't know why I do this. I can hardly believe the words are falling from my lips.

'The water image,' he says knowingly. 'Very important, the water image.'

'It is?'

'You're not an Aquarian, are you?'

'Oh, fuck, please don't tell me that matters.'

'I have no idea. But I like to think it does.'

I don't want this conversation to end and yet it has stalled and neither of know how (or dare) to get it going again. I take giant gulps of beer and John sips at his Pastis.

'So, what's so important about the water image?' I say at last.

'Water is precisely what makes life such an unfathomable

tease. It threatens us as much as it sustains us. It reflects. It absorbs. It corrodes. It preserves. It's what makes us rot. It's what cleans us. It is as gentle as mist and as violent as hail. It is the serenity of a lake and the rage of a torrent. We delight as we frolic on its shores and panic when it sucks us into its depths. We are relieved by its coolness, shudder at its iciness and we sweat and gasp in her steaminess.' He looks up at me. 'What more do you want to know?'

'It moves,' I reply. 'It's always moving.'

'Yes. Always in motion; always seeking the centre of gravity; seeking its own nothingness. It is the beginning of depth and the beginning of height – sea level.'

John pauses and seems quite suddenly sad; almost grumpy. 'I can't say another thing about it. I'm glad you had the image. But I can't speak about it anymore. Words will only crush the meaning out of what you saw. Words crush the meaning out of a lot of things. It's a wonder we rely on them as much as we do.'

'But you're supposed to be a writer!'

He grunts. He suddenly seems enraged. He gulps down his drink, slides a fifty-thousand kip note across the counter and leaves without another word.

Sometimes, I wonder if John Webb is the only person in the world who'll tell me that he hates me.

I don't take Pon that night. I don't take any of them. I drink a lot of beer. I joke with them. They even play The Doors and The Stones and a bit of Jimi Hendrix. I play three games of pool against an Australian and I win all three. This makes me feel inestimably better. Nothing is quite as rewarding as beating an

Australian in some kind of sport.

I veer out of the Destiny Pub and head for the Green Hands Massage Parlour.

I slope along the pavement. People are packing up their cooking stands, stacking plastic chairs, pouring dishwater into the drains. I pick my way through this morass as unobtrusively as possible. Ladyboys in high-heels smoke cigarettes and bicker in the dark shadows of the trees alongside a gas station. Twinkly coloured lights invite patrons into a damp karaoke bar with soft, musty seats. I feel that old cloying helplessness of the real world emerge around me.

It's true that I don't like my name. Never have. Nancy was right about that. Julian! To start with you can't shorten it, except to Jules or Julie. Julian! It's not manly enough. My brother's name was Daniel and everyone used to call him Dan the Man. And then they'd look at me and gawp without words. If you have a son, don't call him Julian. And don't call him Crispin or Tristan or Rupert – strong chance they'll turn out to be gay. Not that there's anything wrong with that, mind you. I'm just saying. And if you call them Hunter or Troy or Jasper, you'll probably land up with a psychopath. And obviously don't call your daughter Gaynor or Dorcas or Leslie.

Nancy had asked whether her name might have defined her. Isn't that the point of names? But she meant something else. If a name *defines* you, what exactly is it? Some kind of brand? I get the feeling that this is what she was asking.

I lie naked on a wooden massage bed. My brittle joints are softened by the booze. The girl rubs my body, my stippled hairy loins and blotchy, swollen ankles with lemongrass-scented oil. I feel it trickling down my crack.

I wonder why they call it Green Hands. Don't they mean green fingers? I picture a plant, a robust species of bean, sprouting from my anus, curling up towards the ceiling. I want to laugh at the image. But then I remember how close I am to crying. I do neither. Instead I clench my jaw and endure the rest of the massage in a grim silence.

At the end of the hour old Julie is aching for a piss.

5

The Russians are back.

They're sitting in the Elephant Bar. It's eleven in the morning and they're enjoying vodka. They seem rather jolly. Ties loosened around their necks as usual.

'Ah, Mr Lockhardt!' says the tall one, the officious, threatening one. 'So good to see you.'

'Hello.'

He stands and walks smartly toward me, putting his hand out. He takes my hand with both of his and presses it firmly. 'You know, I'm glad to bump into you like this.' He releases my hand and ushers me towards their table.

'I … well thank you. I'm glad too.'

'You know, the case of Mr Andropov is resolved. Everything is very perfect. A cardiac infarction. I think that is how you English put it? Yes? He died of a cardiac infarction. A very simple matter. Our consular people have already dispatched the body back to Moscow.'

'I see, well I suppose that is good news. As much as a cardiac infarction can be regarded as good news.'

They all laugh heartily.

'Come, sit with us!' he continues. The others pull out a vacant chair.

'Well, I'm afraid I can't quite, just at the moment. I mean, I'm a bit busy.'

'Oh come now, Mr Lockhardt! We love the Samarang. We come here to enjoy.'

The fact is, that yes, I do want a vodka. I want a vodka more than anything else on earth. And frankly, they're so nice and friendly and I feel great relief that they're no longer accusing me or the hotel for being responsible in some way for the death of their beloved Mr Andropov. I feel helplessly drawn into their collegial circle.

'Well, maybe just one,' I say chummily.

There's a bottle of Stolichnaya on the table. They instantly produce a shot glass and fill it.

'You know?' the tall one says as he takes his seat. 'We did want to say thank you for your help with our investigation. You never know in this day and age. A senior Russian official dies in a hotel in a foreign country. You watch enough CNN to know how crazy it looks, right?'

They all laugh again, just as heartily as before. CNN!

I laugh along with them, but not at all heartily.

'So, our case is finished and we say to you and your team here at the hotel, *thank you*. We were a little bother, no? So thank you!'

I detect in his face something that looks like sincerity. They raise their glasses.

'To the Samarang! *Ura!*' they chime.

We down our vodkas and one of the fat officials reaches for the bottle to refill us all. I want to stand up and leave, but I don't.

I sit there and wait for more vodka.

'You know?' the tall one continues. 'We returned all the bedding. We took the bedding for analysis. But we returned it all. We gave it to the little guy. The little French guy. Sorry, we didn't tell you we took it, but now we return it so, how do you English people say? No harm done?'

They all laugh again and again we toast the Samarang Hotel. '*Ura!*'

The vodka feels good. I feel that comforting burning sensation run through my chest. It's so soothing I think I might want to hang around with this ebullient Russian mob, joking and jesting in a mood of heart-warming international co-operation till the sun goes down. But no. As much as this might be a benign occasion, nothing more than good old-fashioned Russian jollity, I take to my feet.

'Thank you, everyone. I'm glad the investigation is complete and everything worked out so well.'

They stare at me, slightly put out by my prudishness. 'I mean, a cardiac infarction. Thank God for that!'

But my comment elicits a sullen grunt of approval. They can sense my discomfort. I'm being intolerably rude. I don't know where to look.

'Okay, Mr Lockhardt. Very good. You take care now. Okay? Okay?'

'Yes,' I say primly. 'I'll take care.'

I lurch out of the Elephant Bar and head for my office. I close the door behind me, sit in my swivel chair, place my head in my hands and enjoy the slightly numbing effects of the vodka. I know then that if it weren't for the vodka I'd be slitting my wrists with a Stanley knife. I look up and see my amber-coloured glass ashtray on the desk. It runneth over.

Jacques walks in. 'The Russians are here,' he says.

'Yes, I know. I spoke to them.'

'What do they want?'

'They … uhhh … oh I don't know. They said they wanted to return some bedding. They'd taken some bedding from 515. Needed to do some analysis.'

'Yes, I know. A bit strange. But what did they say when you spoke to them?'

'They seemed rather chipper. All drinking vodka. They said they wanted to thank us for our help. Apparently old Andropov died from nothing more spectacular than a bog-standard heart attack.'

'Bog-standard?'

I'd forgotten that Jacques is French. His English is good, but terms like 'bog-standard' would boggle his little Gallic mind.

'I mean a regular heart attack. Nothing suspicious after all.'

Jacques sits down at his desk. With a slightly agitated air he shuffles papers around and begins to staple batches of them together with a strangely bloody-minded fervour. 'Did you ask about the computer? The hard drive for our CCTV? When are they bringing that back?'

I look up and blink at him. 'I forgot. I mean it doesn't matter. Why don't we just get another one? I'll sign the payment voucher and let's just get another one.'

Jacques stops stapling the papers. He looks at me earnestly.

'You should at least have asked them to give it back.' He seems pissed off with me as usual; thinks I'm a cowardly buffoon. 'And it smells like you've been drinking. It's only eleven.'

What an impertinent little fuck! I want to stand up and smack him across the head.

'I had a vodka with the Russians. It's part of the job. We call it relationship-building. You'll get to do this one day when you're senior enough. For now, just stick to the paperwork will you? And enough with the snarky remarks. Try not to make me fire you.'

Jacques has only been at the Samarang for five months. According to his CV he used to work as a financial controller at the Marriott in Paris. He's supposed to be my right-hand man, the one who does the grunt work while I swan about the hotel grounds, grinning at the guests and with my signature *joie de vivre*, putting everyone at ease. But he's an ornery little upstart all right. He'd never be able to carry off such weighty responsibilities. These youngsters today. They think they can do anything. Imbued with so much self-esteem they can barely walk straight; as if they're all on a catwalk in high-heels. Think they're all little Zuckerbergs – super-smart teenagers with their internets and their apps and their unique individual power to change the world.

They don't know shit.

Jacques stands and flounces out of the room. Maybe he'll resign in a great foreign huff. I've had that before. Assistant manager's resigning. The last one did. She was a girl from New Zealand. She took the time to write me a letter accusing me of being a male chauvinistic pig. I laughed and crumpled it up. Now

I'm stuck with Jacques. Be careful what you wish for.

These local kids, they don't have that. They hang around in groups. And they're so polite, so damn respectful of their elders, it makes me want to weep. Remember that? Respecting your elders? There are shopping malls now and the kids hang around them – trying on fashion and cosmetics and buying smartphones, growing into self-actualized self-starters, taking selfies all over the place. If another one of these kids signs up for Facebook I think I'll fucking scream.

I don't want to see this place change. Sometimes I can barely watch a leaf fall from a tree without feeling unsettled.

The thing about this country is that you get the distinct feeling that it has the borders that its neighbours gave it. They haven't had a war with a neighbour for centuries. They had to dodge American bombs; endured some grim times. But they keep the peace here and they don't do it by poking anyone in the eye – like the rest of us. It's as if the existence of this sovereign state depends on something utterly inscrutable, like belief.

Perhaps that's what nations are; have *always* been. They emerge out of nowhere, by dint of some hero on a horse defending a holy site from marauders. Next thing you know there's a kingdom. And an empire. And suddenly it fractures into a hundred pieces, bits seceding, joining up with other bits, overlapping and pulling apart, contracting and expanding, emerging and disappearing.

But now we see this as an aberration – this fluidity. We'll fix these spaces with fortified borders and written treaties; border posts with boom gates; passports and visa application forms; fences, walls, guard-towers and deportation orders. It's as if we've taken the nation – this fluid unstable thing – and set it in concrete; each demarcated zone gets a seat at the General Assembly. We'll protest if anyone fucks with it. We'll get ourselves a Security Council resolution. We'll send our spies, our assassins, our armed forces. We'll intervene. Free will.

John Webb – the old soak – once told me that it's nothing but apartheid on a global scale. We've always been like that. We, as in the West.

But here, in this eternally inscrutable land, they still emerge from their dwellings each morning a little bit unsure as to how the day might end. And they seem fine with that. They don't mess with it. Fate.

So if all this is true then what am I? I like to call myself a colonial orphan. People think this is amusing and so I tell it and retell it at cocktail parties. Born in Rhodesia. Left it as Zimbabwe. Spent my young adulthood in South Africa. I carry a British passport – a legacy left me by my parents. It's an undeserved document. I've only ever been to London once and hated it. Got fleeced at one of those strip clubs in Soho. England must be one of the most sensually austere countries in the world. Right up there with Iran. Who gets fleeced at a strip club; bamboozled by a bully over a bit of boob? What miserly puss could come up with such an idea?

What I mean when I say I'm a colonial orphan is that I'm actually a refugee. Perhaps not stuck in some foreign territory because of war, pestilence or disease. But still, stuck in a foreign territory. Stuck here because the nation that I thought I belonged to – the idea – has simply disappeared. It vanished! Into thin air!

Apartheid on a global scale: geographical zones marked out on a map, special permission needed to move from one to the other. A fiction. Now, a colonial orphan, hunched in a room beneath the elaborate staircase of a grand hotel in the tropics, I recognise, in a moment of wondrous contemplation, that the nation, the essence of it, is just an idea. And ideas – even good ones – are always in motion. None of us are ever quite sure where we stand with ideas. We turn them into ideologies, give each of them a creed, a fixed set of rules. And still they crack and splinter and keep on moving, driving us fucking mad.

But still, we squabble like bitches over the borders. People really fucking annoy me.

That night I think of returning to Destiny. But I don't. I order in. A bacon sandwich with French fries and tomato sauce. I flick between the BBC and CNN and CNBC and Al Jazeera. The alien foetus still squirms in search of freedom on the left side of the screen. They're all talking about the markets and about Syria, BREXIT and Trump. It's Trump and the pornstar, Trump and Korea, Trump and Syria, Trump and Russia. Trump. He's no president. He's clickbait.

And as I flick back and forth between these channels, I feel so suddenly distant from it all. It's all just noise. Aimless noise. Nothing to do with me.

I was married once. A girl called Maureen. She was 23 and I was 28. We produced a daughter called Angela. Maureen has since married a man called Brian. They live on the south coast of Kwa Zulu-Natal, in a place called Shelley Beach. I never hear from her. Occasionally Angela and I exchange an email. She tells me that her mother is happy. They have a house with a view of the sea. They have a boat and a 4x4. She tells me – on the other hand – that she lives with a man called Sean. They have a son called Marcus. They live together in Cape Town. They have produced Marcus out of wedlock. I don't know why that matters.

Maureen and I divorced. I couldn't wait for the day. I was holed up in a beachfront hotel in Durban, waiting for the court order. When my lawyer rang and told me it was done, I ran to the mini bar and finished everything in it. I ran outside and went to the Edward Hotel – the most lavish, most expensive place on the strip – and drank in the bar until I collapsed. Angela was just a schoolgirl then. She used to go to school in her uniform – a green blazer, white shirt and a green chequered skirt – and tell me about all the things she used to do there; how confused she was; how she didn't know what she wanted. I used to grunt and sneer and admonish her for a lack of direction.

After the divorce, she stayed with Maureen. I lived in a one-bedroom flat one block back from the Durban beachfront. I worked as the food and beverage manager of a hotel called the Azure Waters. I used to surf on my days off. I used to smoke pot on the roof of the hotel. I started sleeping with hookers that I picked up from a strip joint in Umgeni Park.

And then I moved to Asia.

It's all become unbearably distant.

I'll never get that back. All that time; all those chances – slipped right through my fingers. My body is already tanking. My face is assuming the shape of a pecan nut. My paunch is weighty, increasingly unmanageable. I can't reach up, can't reach down – not like I used to. My chest aches in the mornings. My fingers are stiffening with gout. My mouth is diseased. My head on fire. I click on health tips. Less of this and more of that. I see these fifty-somethings in their leotards and their luminescent sweaters, jogging with headphones, brimming with satisfaction over their low salt intake. Poor things. They're in denial. Can't face what happens next. They're in a panic. Even so, sometimes I think that they're happier than me. They're making an effort. Got themselves a positive attitude. Sometimes I think I've screwed up. I've screwed up beyond redemption.

Now it's the following afternoon and there's a guy from the Saudi Embassy in the Elephant Bar. Bin-something. Or Fad-something. I forget. I call him 'Mr Saudi' and he thinks I'm very amusing. He spends a lot of time sitting at the counter of the Elephant Bar. He likes to drink expensive Scotch.

'Ah, Mr Saudi!' I say. I'm dressed up to the nines. On my way to the Fuchsia Room, popping in to say hi at the US Chamber of Commerce Annual Ball.

'Mr Julian!' he cries. He seems mightily pleased to see me. He has a beard and dramatically crooked teeth. He wears a shiny, satiny shirt and a heavy gold chain is hanging around his neck. His sweet cologne is overwhelming. 'I'm just here having my relaxing time,' he explains.

'Excellent,' I say. 'It's always good to see you.'

'And for me.'

There's a bit of an awkward pause. I notice patches of sweat under his arms.

'And how is it at the hotel?'

'Oh fine. Excellent. Keeping busy as usual. It's all … just super!'

He laughs generously. 'And no more of the gays?'

It takes me some time to work out what he's talking about. Then I remember. Once – a few weeks back – a gay couple was staying at the hotel. They had a table in the Elephant Bar. One had his hand on the other's knee as they chatted and listened to the piano music. Mr Saudi was outraged. He'd confided in me as I walked by. 'Look at them! It's a violation of the natural order!' he'd said. Now, whenever I see Mr Saudi he likes to remind me about the time we had a gay couple at the hotel. He loves to tell me how gays are a violation of the natural order.

'Ah! Ha ha! No. No more gays. Quite right. So, no trouble there!' I say with my congenial flare intact.

What is it that they do to gays in Saudi Arabia? Burn them at the stake? Or is it something a lot more humane? Execute them by firing squad? Imprison them? Cut off their genitals?

Mr Saudi turns away from me and takes a swig of Scotch, downing it. His hands are quivering and he calls to the barman – a delicate Asian boy called Sam with meticulously combed hair, 'Get me another!'

Then it hits me. He likes Sam! I'd always thought that Sam might swing that way. In fact, it was almost obvious – just from the way he walked. Mr Saudi sits at the bar counter for hours every week, totally love struck by Sam the barman!

'Well,' I say. 'Enjoy your relaxing time.'

'Yes, yes,' Mr Saudi says. Sweat is now pouring down his face.

Ideas. They're in motion.

Quite so, I conclude as I leave the Elephant Bar. I think of my river. It's crashing in a frothy tumult over the rocks; the rapids.

6

The US Chamber of Commerce Annual Ball is a big deal. This is where the captains of industry and all their hangers-on enjoy their big night out. The mining houses and plantation owners, the hydropower executives and the banking giants all gather at the Samarang. People even fly in for the event; from Singapore and Bangkok, Phnom Penh and Ho Chi Minh City. Mountains of Norwegian smoked salmon, bucket loads of Turkmenistanian caviar, truckloads of Californian sparkling wine. It's the most piquant testament to the stunning thrill of free trade. They charge five thousand bucks for a table of ten. Everyone eats too much. They drink too much. It's a lavish affair.

And it would be inexcusable for me not to pop in and say hi on the most profitable night of the year.

The expat community in this town can neatly be divided into three distinct categories: the NGO crowd, the private sector and the French.

True, there are the Russians. I suppose they could be a fourth group, but generally one never sees them, other than at their national day party. Most of the time they hang around that vast embassy compound – barely venture out.

So, tonight it's the private sector and without a doubt, they host the best parties.

I can't tell you how much I enjoy it.

The speeches are all hilarious. The US *chargé d'affaires* is a scream. Leeza or Leena. They even have a compere – a comedian of some repute from Los Angeles. He makes jokes about Harvey Weinstein and Bill Cosby and Donald Trump. We're nearly falling off our chairs. He talks about being high on pot. He talks about climate change and obesity and how you can identify a nascent dictator through his (or her) taste in porn. We have tears streaming down our faces.

I dance. I dance with them all. I'm lithe and sensual. I dance with Leeza or Leena. I dance with Susan from the World Bank. I dance with a girl from India or Sri Lanka or Bangladesh. What does it matter? I dance with another called Mirna or Birna. I feel my paunch shuddering, my buttons at popping point as I gyrate around the floor with stunning agility. I'm nimble and deft as I swirl this way and that, drenched in sweat, eyes ablaze, hands aloft.

And yes! How could I forget! A Moroccan guy tells me he has coke. Imported in a diplomatic pouch! I tell him not to bother being so discreet about it. No need to blow it off the lid of the toilet seat in the restroom. I unlock the Orchid Room. With a groan I lift a giant, gilt-framed mirror off the wall and lay it on the table. 'Here!' I say to him. 'Use the mirror! It's worth ten grand! Nothing better than blowing lines off a ten-grand mirror! Nothing better!'

The Moroccan and his friends burst into laughter. 'I was just kidding!' he says. I see now that he has an unpleasant set of chalky teeth. 'Of course we didn't smuggle it here in a diplomatic pouch!

It was just a joke.' They all think this is terribly funny.

I laugh along with them. 'I suppose the joke is on me! What a funny old trick you've played!'

I'm reddening. I'm fuming. I could hit the Moroccan across the head with a mallet. They think I'm completely unhinged, a complete crackhead. The joke's on me. Ha-fucking-ha.

I return to the ballroom. I take three shots of tequila and I dance. I don't know at that point if I'm dancing with anyone specific, but I dance with such grace, it doesn't matter. I'm inestimably proud of my raw physicality.

Now it's after 4 am and I'm sitting at one of the round tables. By the powers vested in me I have called upon the staff to deliver us a few ashtrays and have proclaimed the Fuchsia Room to be a smoking zone for the rest of the night. I smoke unstoppably. The room is nearly empty. But the music is still pumping. Or is it? I can't really be sure. A group of us is talking. I'm telling jokes. I'm the funniest man alive. I tell them … uh … something about Trump and the size of his hands and … oh, I forget. But it was funny. Let me tell you. It was funny. We were all doubled-up with laughter.

It takes me two days to recover. I emerge in the afternoon of the second day. I walk, forlorn into my office. Jacques has kept the whole place running. I'm inestimably grateful. He's even cleaned out my ashtray.

'Thanks, Jacques,' I say, giving him a tepid pat on the shoulder. 'Haven't been well. Must have been something wrong with that salmon.'

He looks at me doubtfully. He can't quite believe that I'm still employed. Or employable.

'The mirror in the Orchid Room is cracked,' he says with blistering indifference.

'Cracked?'

'Yes. It was an eighteenth-century piece of glass. One of the only artefacts to be recovered from the fire in 1950. It was an eighteenth-century Dutch antique.'

'My God. What a terrible thing.'

'Totally terrible,' Jacques admits.

'Well ... anything on the CCTV? Do we know what happened?'

'I thought you remembered? We don't have CCTV. The Russians took the server.'

'Ah, yes. Well that's a damn shame. Eighteenth century, eh?'

I'm still feeling woozy. Can't handle debauchery as well I used to. The image of the cracked mirror makes me feel slightly sick. It suddenly crosses my mind that I'm about to be fired. Word travels in this miserable fucking town. Maybe Mr Lim has heard about it – the cracked mirror, my amorous advances on plucky ambitious women, my lewd jokes. Could I dismiss it all as 'relationship-building'? How far could I go with Mr Lim? Worst of all, has Jacques had a word in his ear? The treacherous little creep?

That evening I decide to head to Destiny. What I need is a cleansing ale.

And I can hardly believe it when I encounter Nancy at the gate.

'The third time in a row!' I say.

'Yes, like clockwork.'

'It's ... I'm just on my way out.'

'And I'm just on my way in.'

We both laugh.

We both want to know: where am I going and where has she been? Why do we meet at the gate at this time so regularly?

'I'm just on my way for a bit of a ...' I stop. 'A few things to do downtown.'

'I see. Well, I'm just on my way back from the stupa.'

'Oh that stupa!' I say. I'm ready to dismiss it as if it's some mystical Asian thing that has no meaning in the real world. She can sense it. I feel sudden shame. 'I mean, it really is a beautiful thing. Especially, now in the early evening. When the lights are just coming on.'

'Yes. It's beautiful. I like to sit by it in the evenings.'

I wonder what it might be like to sit. To just sit. Sit by something and enjoy it. How do people do that? I feel angst tugging at my throat, reminding me how hard it is to do something as simple as sit still.

'Well,' I say, 'that's lovely. A good idea. Sit by a stupa in the evenings. Lovely.'

We both bid each other farewell. I still think she's a bit fierce. She still thinks I'm a loose cannon. We head our separate ways.

John Webb isn't there.

'Where's John?' I ask the girl. Her name is Cindy.

'He go to South, to Champassak Province.'

'Champassak?'

'Yeah. He like to go to Champassak. He go to mountain. Wat Phou. He go pray.' She laughs. She feels embarrassed. 'You want drink?'

I order a beer and I sit at the counter and I feel as if I miss John – just a bit. I think of the last time we spoke: 'Words crush the meaning out of a lot of things,' he'd said.

The following morning I am back at my desk. I'm pumped and primed and ready for a hard day's slog. Bring it on!

I look at the guest list. The Australian family who had the suite and the adjoining room are checking out. 'Good,' I say. The French couple are checking out too. 'Excellent!' The three Turks and the Latvian are still in residence. We have another delegation of Koreans. A Swiss lawyer who is a guest of the International Finance Corporation. An American actor (there is a note in the comment box telling me that his room is booked by an agent in Hollywood – we're not supposed to know the actor's name). An Indonesian tycoon (there is a note in the comment box telling me that he is lactose-intolerant). A Cambodian tycoon (there is a note in the comment box telling me that he likes dry salted fish for breakfast).

And then I see that one of the American businessmen who'd checked in a few days earlier had requested a move to Room 515. 515? Was that even back in play? I don't recall issuing any executive order. I had the distinctive feeling that the spirit of the dead Russian might well still be active, still bathing in the bath. I didn't like the idea of guests using that room. Maybe in time, yes. But moving that poor American in there seemed indecently hasty.

I call Khek. She enters my office, gives me her usual bow.

'Khek, why have we moved the American, I mean,' I peer at the screen, 'yes, the American to Room 515? I see he was in Room

507. Now he's in 515?'

'He say he want to move.'

'He say?'

'Yes, he say he want to move to 515. He say because of Christian thing. He need to have many "five" in the room number. 507 not enough. 515 better. I say okay.'

'A Christian thing? The number five?'

'Yes.' She reddens and looks at the floor. She's mortified that she might have made some mistake. 'That what he say.' She then faces me with disconcerting defiance.

'Well, yes, I understand. Exactly. Five. Those Christians and their fives! Ha! They love a five. No problem. Thanks for letting me know.'

She returns to her normal colour, gives me an astonishingly bright smile and leaves the room.

We don't have a 55 or 555. Only a 5-0 something or 515. If you like 5's, then 515 is as good as it gets here at the Samarang.

Room 515. For some reason I find this unnerving. This dead Russian thing; it's not going away.

My suspicions are confirmed when Jacques walks in and says, 'There's a guy from the British Embassy in the lobby. He wants to speak to you.'

'What about?'

Jacques gives me a little French shrug. 'Didn't say.'

I don't want to go. I know what this is. It's not about booking an event, or arranging the catering for a function or being invited to a Burns night.

He is sitting in the lobby, next to a Chinese fan palm,

inspecting his fingers. 'Ah, Mr Lockhardt!' he says when he spots me. He smiles.

'Hello.'

He stands. He's a short, reddish, harmless-looking man. He shakes my hand and then walks towards the corridor that leads to the pool. 'I'm grateful for a bit of your time,' he says.

'I always have time for the British Embassy.'

He laughs merrily and continues at a surprisingly strident pace, through the swing doors into the corridor. 'Let's head for the pond at the bottom of the garden. A delightful spot.'

This is an odd remark. It's as if he's trying to cajole me into a picnic.

'Yes,' I say, and after some hesitation I add, 'do you mind telling me who you are?'

He laughs breezily and keeps walking. Stepping onto the pathway that skirts the pool and leads to the pond, he says, 'Charles Brinton'. He stops, turns and shakes my hand again. We proceed towards the pond at a more sedate pace and he resumes conversation in a distinctively quieter voice. 'Look, I'm not going to beat about the bush. You are a British subject and we're looking out for you Mr Lockhardt. That's what we Brits do, isn't it? We look out for each other!' He seems rather proud of this assertion.

'We do?'

He grunts. It's not a question worth answering.

'It seems as if there's a bit of an issue associated with that dead Russian.'

'Mr Andropov?'

'Yes, I believe that's what they call him.' Standing now on the edge of the pond, admiring the morning gleam on the lily pads, he says, 'Our friend, Mr Andropov, so it seems, was here doing a little deal with our Israeli friends. A deal – you understand – that was perhaps not all that agreeable to our Kremlin friends. You know us, we have a lot of friends!' He chuckles and proceeds to walk slowly along the path that encircles the pond. 'Of course, none of this is our business. It's not like us to put our sticky beak into Mr Andropov's financial dealings. Although ...' he pauses. He stops walking and turns to face me. 'It seems as if it's *become* our business. We've received a bit of news that the Russians have got it into their heads that you, Mr Lockhardt, might have removed something from Mr Andropov's safe after he died.'

He doesn't take his eyes off me. This is his seminal moment. He's trained to study every conceivable micro-expression on my face. The scrutiny is unbearable.

I look left. I look right. I look up at the sky. Finally, taking a deep breath I face him squarely and say, 'That's the most ridiculous thing I've ever heard.'

'That's precisely what I thought too.'

'I've been in the hotel business my entire life. I have an unblemished record. I've never stolen anything from anyone in my life! What a fucking load of bullshit!'

'Bullshit indeed, Mr Lockhardt. Still, there you have it. For some reason they have it in their heads and we can't quite be sure what to make of it.' We approach a bench with a view of the pond and Charles Brinton sits down on it leisurely. He crosses his legs and says, 'You probably ought to tell us exactly what's been going here, down at the old ... Samarang.'

I tell him everything. I tell him that Souk and Seng found Andropov dead in the bath. They told Jacques. Jacques told me. I went to the room and there he was, most assuredly dead. I told him how I spotted blood pressure tablets on the dresser and how the bedclothes were unkempt. The Russians arrived and I didn't let them into the room until the police came. They were put out, but I thought it was the right thing to do. Rule of law and all that.

'Quite so,' he agrees.

I tell him about the CCTV footage and how they removed the server.

'And no copies of the surveillance?'

I pause. My hands are shaking. I press them together. I feel sweat pouring from my armpits. 'No. No copies.' I don't want it to be known that had I lied to the Russians; lied to anyone. I'm a hotel manager. I don't go around lying to people. I have an unblemished record.

'Go on,' Charles says.

'The other day they came over again. The Russian Embassy people. They were having vodka in the Elephant Bar. They asked me to join them. Said they wanted to thank me for my help. Turns out Andropov had died of an unremarkable heart attack. Nothing more to it.'

'And you did join them?'

'I ... yes, I did. I had a shot of vodka and then left.'

'Ah!' Charles Brinton smiled and looked calmly at the pond. 'So that's how they did it.'

'Did what?'

'Lifted your prints. Lifted your prints from the vodka glass.'

My heart sinks. Adrenalin fizzes through my veins. 'I thought that only happened in the movies.'

'Where do you think we get all our best ideas?' He laughs briefly. 'Still, it seems this is what they have on you. They seem to think you meddled with the safe in Andropov's room. They have your prints.'

'But I didn't meddle with the safe! I didn't do anything of the sort!' I say hotly.

'No, it would seem so.'

'Exactly.'

Charles Brinton continues to survey the pond. 'Well, you've been very helpful, Mr Lockhardt. I appreciate your candour.' He stands. 'And you might not have any suspicions about our Israeli friend? None of us can fathom who it is.'

'Your Israeli friend? No, I don't. I don't think we've had any Israelis here for a while. I don't remember seeing any. I mean, seeing anyone who, you know, looks Israeli.'

'You mean no one wandering around in a yarmulke?' He laughs.

'Exactly.'

We commence our walk back to the hotel. 'Well I'd hate to think that you might be in some kind of danger, Mr Lockhardt. Just sit tight for the moment. No sudden moves. We're doing what we can. Looking into it. These things have a way of ... you know, panning out.'

'Panning out! I'm not entirely sure what that means.'

'It'll all be fine. Here,' he says, reaching into his top pocket, 'my card. You call me anytime, if anything else comes to mind.'

I look at the card. Charles Brinton: Economic Affairs Advisor. British Embassy.

'And you'll keep our little conversation under wraps, won't you?'

'Of course.'

We reach the top of the path, about to step into the corridor and he turns. 'About that unblemished record of yours, Mr Lockhardt.'

'Yes?'

'Well ... it's not that unblemished is it?'

'I ... it ... what do you mean?'

'Weren't you fired from the Azure Waters in Durban all those years ago?'

I redden. 'Oh, that! Well, the thing was, I mean ...'

'Something to do with you and narcotics and prostitutes, if I've got my facts right.'

I don't reply. I am silenced by an unspeakable rage.

'It's very important that you play this with a straight bat, Mr Lockhardt. We are on the same side, after all.'

I follow Mr Brinton back to the lobby. He turns on his heel and says, 'Great to see you again, Julian. We'll call you about the catering arrangements!' He shakes my hand and walks away.

I look around the lobby. Why did he say that? One of the Americans – the one that looks like Harrison Ford – is sitting on a bench, staring at an iPad. And the three Turks are standing together near the concierge desk, waiting – apparently – for a taxi to arrive.

I run to my office and throw up in the sink. And then it feels as if I need a shit. Urgently. I run to my room, slide to a stop outside the door, rush inside and evacuate with stunning relief.

No. I haven't been feeling that well lately.

7

'How was the South? Didn't you go to Champassak?' I say to John.

'I love the South,' he replies.

It's been a week; a not-very-easy week either. I've been on edge. I've been surly with the staff. I even told Jacques to go and fuck himself.

At least I haven't seen any more Russians. So that's a good thing.

'Cindy told me that you go to pray on a mountain top.'

John ignores me. Seems as if he doesn't want to talk about praying or mountaintops. 'I love the South,' he says again. 'I love the Middle. I love the North. Laos. It's the last bit of original Asia left. The rest of them have sold up. But not Laos. Although the Chinese are building a high-speed railway right through the middle. I hate to see this place change.'

'Me too.'

'But change it must, I suppose. They'll handle it. Impermanence. They handle it better than most.'

After a long pause my curiosity gets the better of me and I persist: 'So, is it true? Did you pray on a mountain top?'

John glares at me with disconcerting severity. 'What the fuck is it to you?'

I feel sore. I like John. I want him to like me back. Just one fucking miserable human being on the face of this wretched planet to like me, to comfort me! Just one! Is that so much to ask?

I return to what I think is a more agreeable subject, our affection for Laos. 'I like Laos too. Don't get me wrong. Apart from the law that prohibits foreigners from bonking the local girls.'

'A damn fine idea,' John confirms with an emphatic nod of his head. 'Keeps the sex tourists out. Middle-aged divorcees who use hair-colouring. Just like you.'

What the fuck is it with John Webb that he gets to be such a prick?

'I don't colour my hair!' I protest.

'Oh yes you do. It's obvious. It has that shiny, purplish hue to it. It's obvious. Hair colouring! Never looks right. It's by fraudsters for fraudsters.'

'Fuck you, John.'

I storm out of Destiny. John Webb isn't a big man. I could easily throttle the little prick. I'm in a blind old rage. I barrel into one of the leaky karaoke bars. I take a room and three cheap, slightly plump girls sit with me on the sofa. I finish a bottle of Johnnie Walker. I throw up in the squat toilet at the back of the room. I order another bottle. It's true, I do use hair colouring. I like it jet black! How the hell can he tell? The prick! I try to sing a Tom Jones number. I'm in the mood for a heart attack. A big beautiful, throbbing, hurt-like-hell cardiac infarction!

I leave the girls. I leave them money. They laugh and admire me. The fucking bitches! The street outside is whirling around me. I veer towards a tuk-tuk driver on the corner. Weed. That's what I want! I want to smoke on the rooftop of the Samarang!

Just like I used to! I want to go back in time! I drop by a mini-mart and buy some rolling papers. I'm massively excited! Reeling and weaving along darkened streets I head back to the hotel with clear purpose.

To get to the rooftop of the Samarang I have to take the elevator to the sixth floor. The doors open with a ping and I lurch along the corridor, a dark hulking figure, advancing like death for the fire door at the end. I spot something in the gloom. A great black, crumpled heap in the passage. It looks like a bin bag. What the fuck is that thing?

As I draw nearer, I see the legs splayed out and I peer over it. Her greyish face looks up at me. Her dark, shimmering eyes blink at me. I hear her make a tiny squeak.

'Nancy!' I roar. 'Nancy Bacon, you're drunk!'

She blinks again, unable to utter another sound.

'You're fucking drunk in a heap on the fucking floor! Jesus fucking Christ, well how about that?'

No, I don't like Nancy Bacon either. Nancy and her fucking view of the stupa. Hard-nosed bitch.

I laugh. I step over her and I reach the fire door at the end without sparing her another thought. I use my keys to open the door without setting off the fire alarm. I'm surprised I can do that. I slam the door behind me and walk to the edge of the building. The lights of this humid little town twinkle at me from behind a greyish film of smog. I lie back on the concrete surface, pull a plastic bag of weed from my pocket. I try to roll a joint, but it's all become insufferably complicated and I fall asleep next to a pool of vomit and with tears pouring down the sides of my face.

8

I am put on an 'extended leave of absence'.

This has been arranged by Jacques after conferring with Mr Lim. Firing me outright seemed to be a more complicated option for reasons that aren't all that clear to me.

Mr Lim does not take any of my calls. I am relieved, quite frankly. I like Mr Lim; couldn't bear the idea of letting him down. Jacques, my assistant manager, has now, somehow, assumed command of the hotel. It's what he always wanted. He has no doubt convinced Mr Lim of his unswerving dedication to the business and how – given recent unfortunate events – he will magnanimously, even reluctantly, assume the weighty burden of leadership.

He informs me, in his usual prim manner, of the arrangements. 'I explained to Mr Lim that you are overworked. Stressed. Burned out. I haven't told him anything more.'

Anything more?

They had found me baking in the midday sun on the rooftop of the hotel. My little bag of weed had burst open and its contents were scattered amongst the mosses. I was sunburnt, dehydrated and had a cracking headache. There was, of course, no CCTV footage of my arrival at the hotel that night. But I was the prime suspect in their investigation as to who had urinated in one of the elevators. I had also apparently told Farr, the dainty Nepalese night manager to go and hang himself.

But worst of all, it was how I treated Nancy Bacon that galled my accusers.

No, Nancy Bacon was not in a drunken heap on the floor. I ought to have recalled that when she'd checked in she'd said she didn't drink. We'd even had tea sent up to her room because she had declined my offer of a free cocktail in the Elephant Bar. I ought to have remembered that.

No, Nancy was not drunk. She was sick. Nancy Bacon has cancer. She'd collapsed in the passage on her way to her suite. Her legs had given out. She is riddled with tumours.

I had to clear out my room. Best not to be seen around the hotel. Now I am living in a small villa, not far from the river. Mr Lim apparently insisted on it. 'He said we should take care of you,' Jacques explained. I can hear Mr Lim say this. 'You take care Mr Juwy, okay? Ah good, good.'

In a way, Jacques is right. I am burnt out. I feel like I'm burnt out for good. But Jacques tells me that this is a temporary arrangement, 'until ... how do you English say it? Get your shit together?' But I'm not so sure it's a temporary arrangement. It's obvious that Jacques would prefer it to be permanent. 'I mean, the alternative is that you could simply resign. Go home.'

Home? What does that even mean? The United Kingdom? To the sovereign that deigned to issue me with a passport? On its cover page she beseeches the other sovereigns (each of them in charge of some kind of ethnic, religious or ideological supremacy) to let me pass without let or hindrance. That's the way the world works. They'll have me shot if I'm in the wrong place without the right papers.

Or Zimbabwe? The place of my birth. But it's just a place on a map. I know nothing of those people – beating their infernal fucking drums! That was the whole point of living there. They were supposed to learn all about us; fall about praising us. Not the other way around. That was the idea; the unifying idea. That was the nation. It wasn't even called Zimbabwe when I was born. Jacques is so young he probably doesn't even know that. He tells me that Zimbabwe has a new president; that things are looking up. Jesus! He really wants me out of here!

The world has conspired against me – the colonial orphan.

Home. No. I have little money. I have no new ideas. I feel bad about Nancy. What a big fat puss I am!

I'm supposed to stop drinking too. This is what they tell me.

Of course, I don't stop. That would be ridiculous. When a man runs out of ideas, the last thing he should do is stop drinking. So, I sit at home – at the borrowed villa – and I drink on the sofa whilst watching TV. Thank God for Trump. It's the greatest show on earth! The perfect entertainment for people who have run out of ideas.

The news used to be the most boring thing on TV. It was for political hotheads and people who had some obscure fascination in the most tiresome issues: public expenditure, social welfare, human rights, taxation policy, the imprecision of electoral maps. They were all bookish creatures. But now we all watch it. We all get to think we're a bit bookish – while we sit on our sofas, eating corn chips and laughing at Trump and all the hookers who want to sue him and how he calls the leader of North Korea 'little rocket man'.

I want to phone Angela. I want to know how she is. Fuck, I even want to phone Maureen. Hey Maureen, how're you doing these days? How's Brian? He's doing great? Oh fantastic! Hey Maureen, remember the time we had sex in that little Datsun? With the sun going down? Katrina and the Waves on the radio? Fuck, I'll never forget that. Best day of my life! Yours too? What? You're kidding me! That's great!

But it's not to happen.

I wonder what Angela's son is like. Marcus. Does he look like me? Just a little? Jet black hair? And why did they call him Marcus? It's not a family name. But still, it's better than Julian. That's for sure.

Sometimes I go up to the deli around the corner and I buy supplies. They sell French cheese and Spanish pickles and Italian wine. It's not bad. Fuck me if I don't bump into Mr Saudi there one afternoon.

'Hey, Julian!' He seems inexplicably happy. And then his expression falters, becomes decidedly grim. 'I mean, how are you? I heard you haven't been well.'

'No, not well, Mr Saudi. You know how it is. I'm fine. Just not well. You know. That sort of thing.' I know I'm not making any sense. But at least the nasty little prick is being nice.

'Oh well, get well soon, heh? We like to see you back at the hotel. Always love to see Julian there when I'm having my relaxing time.' He leans towards me. I'm sickened by that cologne. 'We make joke about all the gays there, right?' He grins.

'We do? Oh great. Yes. The gays.'

As I amble listlessly back to my villa, my shoulders drooping with the weight of Spanish pickles, I secretly hope that Sam the barman, the delicate object of Mr Saudi's desire, has an elephantine-sized cock. I hope Sam splits that fat odious Arab in half. I hope it hurts like hell.

I think about Nancy every day. I vaguely remember stepping over her. I remember her eyes blinking at me in the dark. She was unable to utter a sound. Poor thing was in agony, waiting for another member of the human race to happen by and comfort her. I remember saying something outrageously nasty to her.

And she had repeatedly told me that she wasn't here to *enjoy* the stupa. But she was grateful to be near it. What did that mean? She was at the Buddhist ceremony when they had a go at coaxing Mr Andropov's spirit out of Room 515.

And now I am reminded of my river.

In the gloaming – it's a time of unimaginable beauty – I walk to the stupa. A few mopeds whir around it. A tuk-tuk rattles past. Small bats dart this way and that against an inky sky.

There she is. She's in a wheelchair. Hunched in silence near the stupa. I walk towards her. She looks up at me. Her face is sunken, her eyes set in darkness, her feisty, squarish frame, now crumpled in that seat. I fall to my knees and sob uncontrollably.

After a very long time – I cannot bare to look at her – she pats me gently on the shoulder and says, 'It's all right, Mr Lockhardt.'

She has an assistant. He's a thin but muscular Asian man and he emerges from the gloom and wheels her back to the hotel.

I walk – strangely calm – back to my borrowed villa and sleep as if it's the first time I've done that in years.

I return to the stupa the following evening.

I approach her; hear my feet tread on the dry grass. She does not move. I sit on the grass next to her. We are silent. Every now and again I feel a sob rising in my throat, tears pricking the corners of my eyes.

After a long time her helper emerges and wheels her away.

I continue to sit there. I hear the night beetles. I study the blackened fronds of the ferns that grow and die in the shaded cracks of the plinth.

And the following evening I return again.

I sit in the same place. The silence between us is as tangible as the humidity. Sometimes I regard it as a kind of damnation. I want to defy it; blurt something out; make some inane sound; offer explanations and opinions; return to the voluble cursing routines of the human race. Sometimes I regard it as a kind of anaesthetic. It is numbing.

I sense it is almost time for Nancy to leave. I sense the presence of her helper standing somewhere close behind us.

She says, 'I've come here to die.'

This is a dramatic thing to say and I feel words rising up; a compulsion to speak: oh no, that can't be, true! But I say nothing.

'I was born here,' she continues. 'Across the street. I was born in that house across the street. It's a dental surgery now. Do you see it?'

Across the street is a neon sign. An image of a large white tooth with pinkish roots glimmers over the square. Phong's Dentiste.

'I was born in that house in 1966. My father was a Swedish diplomat. My mother was Khmu. One of the ethnic minorities from the North. We lived in that house until 1975 – just after the revolution. One night, as my brother and I slept in our beds, my parents came in and carried us to a waiting car outside. We were driven to the airport in our pyjamas. I remember holding my father, my arms around his neck. I was crying. I kissed him on the face. He handed me to my mother and we hurried through the airport. Boarded a plane for Hong Kong. That was the last time I saw him.'

I look across at Nancy. She is fixed, trance-like in her chair.

'The Khmu people say that we should die in the place we are born. This is to acknowledge the cycle to which we are inescapably bound. So, that is why I'm here. I am foolish. Or perhaps I am brilliant. Here, honouring the traditions of my ancestors.'

'But ... but, treatment. What about treatment? I mean, couldn't you, you know, get to a hospital in Bangkok? They have the most amazing facilities down there. I saw a news item the other day. Gene therapy. I mean, cancer isn't what it used to be.' I suddenly shut up. I feel as if the entire universe can't handle another word from Julian Lockhardt; it would simply implode in exasperation if I made even the tiniest squeak.

It's hard to tell in the darkness, but I suspect she is smiling slightly.

'Oh,' she says. 'Cancer has its place.' She summons her helper and they depart.

The following evening I ask her, 'Can you tell me what happened to your father? Why was it the last time you saw him?'

'Oh, you want to know my story?'

'I suppose I do.'

She smiles, still looking at the stupa. After a pause she says, 'If you sit here for long enough and don't make a sound, that's exactly what will happen. You will find yourself interested in stories. Your story. My story. Their story. The first thing you will realise is that it's all one story. It's our story.'

She turns her head to face me. This causes her to wince slightly. 'That's why it's so hard to sit in silence. We must let go of our solitary, singular experience and rejoin the others; all of them, the ones we've met along the way; the ones we've resented, even hated.'

It is my turn to wince. I am reminded of the resentment and yes, even hatred, with which I had once regarded her. That familiar painful lump returns to my throat. A gentle breeze sweeps silently across the forecourt. A bullfrog begins to squawk in the reeds. My river returns.

'No one really knows what happened to my father. The Swedish Embassy had already closed and he'd lost his diplomatic immunity. He'd defied Stockholm's instructions to return home. In the 80s the Swedish government tried to find out what had happened to him. There was some suggestion that he was secretly helping the Americans. I suspect he was. They found a record of him as a prisoner. Eventually, in 1987 he was released. They sent him back to Stockholm. He had a heart attack on the plane. Was dead on arrival.'

'I'm very sorry.'

'He was a very political man. We've all become very political,

I suppose. It won't do us any good.'

The following evening, as I walk along the riverside towards the stupa, a strong wind blows. It picks up dust and grit and has it swirling in great squalls through the air. There are flecks of foam on the river as the wind tries to whip it back upstream. Lightning bolts shimmer on a burnt out horizon and giant storm clouds cast a portentous gloom over the city.

Nancy has a head-scarf and her helper stands by the wheelchair. I'm too late.

'It's the first of the monsoons,' I yelp.

'Yes, quite a storm,' she agrees. 'We'll be getting back now, Julian. The rain will be pelting down any minute.'

'Yes, of course. Good idea.'

I stand next to the stupa and watch her being wheeled away through the whorls of dust that dance about her like phantoms. They stop and she turns with effort. 'Julian!' she cries.

I run up to them.

'Do you have a car?'

'A car? Uh. No. No, I don't.'

'Oh,' she pauses thoughtfully. 'Well, you have a license, don't you? I mean you can drive?'

'Yes. I can drive.'

'Good. We can get a car from the rental company. Come to see me at the hotel tomorrow. We'll go for a drive. I want to show you something. And pack a bag. We'll be gone for a while.'

9

I am sitting in a brand new Toyota Fortuner. It has the new-car smell. It's high up off the ground and I feel emboldened sitting in the driver's seat. I haven't driven a car in years. This is empowering.

Nancy sits in the front passenger seat and her helper, who I now know goes by the name of Wai Ming, sits in the back seat behind her. If it weren't for his grey speckled hair, I would have said he was about twenty-eight. That's the thing with Asians. They age so much better than us. Until they get to ninety when they suddenly look as if they're a hundred-and-five. Still, it's not a bad deal. I won't be getting to ninety.

We're off on a road trip! I'm so excited I feel like a drink. But Nancy has said no drinking and driving, so that'll have to wait.

It was odd walking into the hotel that morning to pick her up. Jacques had stood in the lobby staring at us with his mouth hanging open.

'But you hate Nancy Bacon!' he'd said.

'I know. It's my secret plan. I'm taking her up north to drown her in a river. No one need ever know, except you, my trusted underling, and me.'

'And driving? I mean, you're okay to drive. No more drinking?'

Once more I'd thought of hitting him across the head.

When Wai Ming wheeled Nancy out into the lobby there was

something of a commotion. The bellman had followed with a trolley-load of baggage and scant regard for anyone in his way. People leapt and dithered as his giant trolley surged through the room. Sith had jumped from his stool to open the swing doors and Jacques stood with his hands on his hips, still with his mouth hanging open.

I'd noticed the events signboard perched next to one of the sofas: Welcome to the Inter-Ministerial Regional Dialogue on Commercial Fisheries. Now that sounded like fun. Sounded like something worth jetting in for. I thought of all the well-rehearsed verbiage. This was dialogue on an industrial scale. There was money to be made out of it.

Now we are driving on the northern road, up into the mountains – to Khmu country.

'They've got a CD player,' I say with delight. 'And a thing for a USB stick.' But none of us has a CD or a USB stick, so music – holiday tunes – won't be a part of the experience.

I learn that Wai Ming is in the business of palliative care. He's a fifty-year-old Singaporean. He'd once taken a course in Sweden on craniosacral therapy, which is where he'd met Nancy. They've been friends for nearly twenty years. Now he's taking care of her. I can't tell if this is a commercial arrangement. I want to ask, but I don't.

In all the six years I've lived in this country I've hardly ventured out of Vientiane. When I was newly arrived, I once went south to a waterfall for a picnic with a girl I'd befriended from the Destiny Pub. That didn't work out so well. And I once went on a lamentable 'team-building' weekend with hotel staff to the banks of a hydroelectric reservoir. We went on a boat trip, singing karaoke. It was lamentable because a large number of the staff resigned the following week for reasons that I've never been able to fathom.

Now it's Nancy, Wai Ming and me.

The outskirts of the city are a calamitous blend of brownish rice paddy and pinkish land fill, small, but ornate hotels that sell rooms by the hour and businesses that sell sheets of aluminium and blue plastic pipes and bags of cement. Mopeds whizz past on either side of us. Cows amble almost aimlessly along on the crumbling edges of the road, sniffing at the red dust; their hooves speckled with mud. It's like this for miles. Gradually, it becomes apparent that all the commercial bustle is just a thin strip that hugs the edges of the road and beyond that are the sunken rice paddies, drained and brown before planting. Beyond the paddies are thickets of old forest.

Nancy has taken out a map and unfolded it on her lap.

'So, tonight we'll stay in Vang Vieng. I've been there before. It's a sweet, messy little town. You'll like it. Tomorrow we'll head up into the hills. Up to Pho Daeng. It's my mother's village.'

It all sounds mightily exotic and exciting and as I press my foot against the accelerator, savouring the power of the big car, I am also mindful of how good I feel. I haven't felt this way in years and I never want this to end – me and my time with a terminally ill cancer patient and her solemn Singaporean helper.

I become frantically chatty. I tell them about the time I learnt to drive and how I crashed into the back of a tractor. I tell them about how my brother and I used to go to my uncle's farm outside

Salisbury and catch barbel and one time, after hooking something large and powerful and struggling with it for hours, I hauled in a steel fold-up chair! I tell them about the time we took our Shona maid to a modern shopping centre and how she ran away from the escalators. It was the first time she'd seen such a monstrous thing. She said it had the skin of a snake! I tell them about my marriage to Maureen and the birth of my daughter, Angela. I say that Maureen and I divorced. It was amicable. We're the best of friends!

I notice that Nancy occasionally drifts off to sleep. This makes me talk even more. As we begin an ascent over a range of low, forested hills she begins to groan and whimper. Her eyes are closed. It seems as if she's shivering.

'I think we'd better pull over,' Wai Ming says.

I draw the car to a halt and Wai Ming jumps out to open her door. I watch him hold her wrist – a grey, almost translucent limb – and expertly administer a shot of morphine.

Nancy sinks back into her seat. We recommence with our journey and she says, 'Go on. I'm listening.'

Vang Vieng is a small town on the edge of a river. Beyond that is a range of limestone peaks. In the slanting afternoon shadows a man with a pointy hat is wading through a flooded paddy. This is the Asia that I'd imagined when I was a kid. I'm glad I get to see it; that it's still here. In Laos.

We check into the Vang Vieng Riverside Lodge. Wai Ming and Nancy share a twin room and I have a room to myself.

'Right, so let's all meet at the bar on the verandah for a drink. Sun's almost gone!'

They nod. We go our separate ways. Here I am in a hotel room of my own. I'm a guest. I turn on the TV. Something about Syria. I turn it off. I go to the bathroom which is distinctively musty. I turn on the light and an army of mosquitos springs into flight. Still, the room is comfortable enough. I've had my fair share of bad hotels: cockroaches under the pillowcase, copulating rodents in the ceiling, condoms under the bed, blood on the walls. But here, this room is pleasant enough. It has its own tiny packages of soap and tiny bottles of shampoo-conditioner. It has a minibar containing two bottles of ozone-treated drinking water.

Vang Vieng once enjoyed some infamy as a place for backpackers loaded with pills. They partied along the banks of the Nam Song River. They floated on tyre tubes, sozzled out of their sunburnt heads, down the river like in one of those deranged scenes from *Apocalypse Now*. Each year a few of them drowned. I recall one year was particularly deadly. 'A bumper crop!' so John Webb had described it. We'd both laughed out loud. But the town has cleaned up its act since then. New multi-storey hotels with swimming pools and floral-scented spas are being built on the banks of the river. Soon, you'll be able to get here in the comfort of a Chinese high-speed train. The backpackers will drift off somewhere else, in search of cheap thrills. But cheap thrills in faraway exotic lands are rare these days. Perhaps backpacking is finished. Too many people are doing it, or *have* done it. And in their wake are luxury resorts, wine bars serving imported oysters, golf courses and freshly built airports.

I lie on the bed for less than a minute. I blink at the ceiling and then I run to the verandah on the edge of the river and I order a beer.

The sun is well down by the time Wai Ming arrives and I'm well onto my fourth or fifth or sixth beer.

'Wai Ming!' I say. I'm nearly apoplectic with excitement. 'Just in time for a drink!'

He smiles at me dimly and pulls up a chair. 'I've got Nancy a bit to eat. She'll stay in the room. You know, she gets tired easily.'

I feel a bit flattened. 'Yes, of course. I mean, you know …'

Wai Ming orders a passionfruit shake.

'You don't … I mean … drink?'

He gives me that familiar dim smile and says, 'Not much.'

'Huh!' I grunt. 'My father always used to say that you can't trust a man who doesn't drink.'

'So, he used to drink did he?'

I turn away from Wai Ming and face the sparkling surface of the dark river. I can't really remember if my father drank. I don't think he did. I suddenly don't feel like talking about it.

I order a fried rice with pork and he orders stir-fried vegetables with steamed rice. I notice that before we start eating he seems to be seized by some strange kind of trance. It's as if he's saying some kind of grace.

He tells me a bit more about his friendship with Nancy.

'I was in Sweden. I was interested in energy treatments. I was quite swept up in a lot of hype. Used to go to conferences and retreats all over the world. Listened to lectures by the gurus in the business. They were all a bit sure of themselves. I didn't notice that until I was standing at a tram stop in Stockholm on my way back to my hotel. I was holding a book called *The Masks of Energy and the Truth Beyond*. Nancy happened to be standing next to me and she said: "That seems to be quite a long book for what I'm sure is a fairly simple subject."' Wai Ming smiles at the memory of it. 'She had a curious way of looking at me. A crooked smile. I took her to be a sceptic of energy treatment and was all set to challenge her. I was sure that I could prove something. So I offered her a session – a free craniosacral session. She took me to her hotel and lay down on the bed.'

At this point I blink with astonishment. I've heard this sequence before.

'No, no, nothing like that,' Wai Ming laughs quietly. 'I performed the treatment. Afterwards I asked her how she felt and she said, "Different". That was all. And so I asked her, well, do you believe me now? Do you believe that energy treatment works? And she said, "I'm sure it works. I'm just not sure we know what it means." I was silenced by that remark. When I returned to my conference the next day her words stuck with me. I watched therapists from all over the world – California, Chile, Bali, Japan – all telling me about what it means if a patient visualizes royal purple or if they hear voices or feel twitches in their fingers. It means they're short on crystals. It means they are destined for greatness. It means they've been given a hard time of it. Or so they said. It suddenly hit me that it was all a bit of a fraud. So I returned to Singapore and I went into palliative care. That's what I've done for twenty years – thanks to Nancy.'

I am not sure about the royal purple, the crystals or the twitches. I have vague recollections of that kind of stuff from bits I've seen on TV – bits that I've easily channel-surfed over.

But somehow, what Wai Ming says makes some kind of sense. I think a lot of things are fraudulent. People are – by and large – fraudulent.

'Nancy always had a strange take on the truth,' Wai Ming explains. He is unexpectedly conversational 'I think she always understood the truth – the meaning of it, even the purpose of it – to be a bit fluid. It moves. It's not something that can be seized or clung onto or explained away by some sort of immutable formula or sustained by some kind of impeccable logic. It is instead revealed to us by the tumult of our emotional experience of life. It resides inside us. The rest is ignorance. Even knowledge is another kind of ignorance. Standing on its own, a huge body of knowledge has no meaning. It's just data. You can process it in an orderly way, like a computer. But the meaning of it, the value of it, is only revealed when some erratic, emotional creature tries to interpret it. And in any case, to know something is to grasp something in a fixed unchanging way. It excludes all the other possibilities; the various shifting perspectives of perception and by that process of exclusion it becomes, itself, a body of ignorance.'

Knowledge is ignorance? What the hell did they put in that passionfruit shake?

I grunt with indifference, hoping he'll change the subject.

He takes a final gulp of steamed vegetable with a dab of soya sauce. He chews it with a thoughtful expression as if it's the first thing he's ever eaten. 'Up early tomorrow,' he says. 'Long way to Pho Daeng.'

'Yes!' I agree with an emphatic nod of my addled head.

As soon as he disappears around the corner, I head back to

the bar and buy a bottle of Scotch, just before they turn the lights off.

The following morning Wai Ming and Nancy have already enjoyed a cool morning stroll around the town. Of course, they hadn't actually *strolled*. Wai Ming had wheeled Nancy around on her wheelchair. They had breakfasted and spent some time on the verandah muttering over when I, their driver, might emerge from his room.

Still, they had to knock on my door eventually and insist that we move on.

This all disappoints me because I'd rather liked Vang Vieng and had hoped to spend a bit of time exploring the town, the river, the rice paddies and the limestone peaks. Booze! This is what you miss out on! This is what they always tell me.

I'm still chipper when we get into the car and get going, but I carry with me a rather weighty suspicion that this won't last. I'm beset by a grave – and gravely familiar – reminder of my many appalling inadequacies. I start to doubt if I can even keep this huge car properly under my control. My hands are trembling slightly and this makes me grip at the steering wheel with a fervour that slowly exhausts me.

I press my foot against the accelerator. The road is windy and treacherous. Huge lorries and buses swerve around the bends, hogging the narrow road. But I am defiant, eager to exaggerate the control I have over this modern vehicle. Nancy eventually cries, 'Slow down, you oaf!'

I instantly plummet into a state of despair. I can't believe she spoke to me like that. It's the old Nancy. The old Nancy who demanded her room with a view of the stupa!

I say nothing. Words – remonstrations and retorts – remained trapped in my head, never to be uttered. My throat aches.

I am compelled to drive this powerful machine at a stupidly low speed – as if I'm manoeuvring a giant tea trolley, stacked with teetering cakes, rattling with china plates, through these wild mountain passes. I approach each corner with gingerly trepidation. I am hampered by the demands of a sick old woman and her slightly sanctimonious companion. I stop for another morphine shot – hers, not mine. I circle the vehicle, aggressively smoking a cigarette. My old holiday swagger has abandoned me.

Now we continue, even more slowly than before. The road is steep and the bends are exacting. I drive in a dismal silence.

Nancy says, 'I don't suppose I mind if we race over the edge of a cliff and die in an inferno at the bottom of a valley. I mean, why should I care? I haven't got long to go and I suppose a car accident is as good a way to go as any. It's just that I want to get to my village, Pho Daeng, and more specifically, the mountain of Phou Nang Fa. That's what I want. So it'd be a shame if we didn't make it.'

'A shame? Dying in an inferno would be a *shame*?'

She lets out a sigh. She is defeated by my question and I feel a bit bad about it.

'It doesn't matter,' I say. 'I've got the point.'

I continue to drive with ridiculous caution. I feel irritable and hamstrung and I'm not enjoying the journey anymore.

Wai Ming and Nancy: they're friends. Been friends for twenty years. Met in Stockholm. Had this incredible almost nonsensical bonding experience. It's me against them.

And what does she mean when she says that all she wants is to visit Phou Nang Fa? She knows what she wants? What *do* we want? I've always struggled with this question. Even now, as I drive this monstrous car along sweeping mountain bends, I'm not so sure. I want to be down at Destiny Pub beating Australians at pool. I want to laugh with the girls; their silly jokes. I want Pon in my bed. I want orgasms. I want cigarettes.

We stop again for another round of morphine. Nancy and her morphine and me and my cigarettes!

It's cool outside now. We're at a distinctively higher altitude.

'So,' I say, as the journey resumes. 'Why do you want to come up here, to Phou Fa Na or whatever it's called?'

Nancy looks out the window. 'It's Phou Nang Fa and to speak truthfully, I don't know if it is what I want. I suppose what is so irritating about wanting something is that wrapped up somewhere in all that desire is the realisation that wanting something is the same as not wanting it.'

I feel a bit sorry for asking the question. Her answer isn't much of an answer. It's one of those remarks that goes nowhere; yields no useful conclusion.

She turns to face me. She gives me a crooked smile – it's becoming a familiar expression. 'But at least we're here. Driving around. Isn't that enough?'

Actually, it is enough. In the valleys are wild banana trees and the gorges are thickly forested. Some of the hills have jagged rock faces, water slipping down their blackened sides. Mist hangs in the crevices. It's a place of astonishing beauty. In any other part of the world it would be crammed with tour buses.

'True enough, I suppose. But why ... why the mountain, Phou-whatever? I mean, specifically. We're not just here to drive around are we?'

'Phou Nang Fa? Well some might say that it has something to do with my ancestors. My mother was born in Pho Daeng. It overlooks the mountain. I was curious about her life and that's what brought me here about ten years ago. But that's not really the reason we're here now. When I look back at my life I see only a few places in the world where I have been strangely moved – strangely aware, comforted even, by mortality.'

'Comforted by mortality?'

She laughs drily. 'You seem shocked.'

'I am a bit.'

'Some people call these experiences spiritual. I'm not sure if that is what they are. That seems too specific. I like to call them mysterious. Beyond knowledge. I'm not sure they deserve much more of an explanation.'

I still have some of that Scotch from the night before packed into my bag. That's a spirit! That's not knowing! Beyond knowledge! She could simply have downed a bottle of Scotch instead of driving all the way out here in search of mystery.

Still, here we are, driving around. The scenery is admittedly spectacular and we're okay.

She adds, 'I suppose whether you call it spiritual or whether you call it mysterious, this ... this kind of awareness is what counts. It's what makes the whole thing bearable.'

'You suppose?'

She turns to me again, with that same crooked smile and says, 'I don't know, Julian. We'll find out though, won't we?'

Nancy is one of those esoteric people that I've never taken much of a liking to. I'd never suspected that about her. I'd thought her to be a bit more like me – a bit cynical, a bit fed up; angered by how much pain goes into the production of an unremarkable life. But here she is talking about ancestors and spiritual awareness and how a distant mountain grants her a comforting sense of mortality. Those esoteric types don't normally get angry. I find them annoying. They smile way too much. They bow and dip their heads with a sort of smugness that suggests they've found the Middle Way, while the rest of us shilly-shally about like a right bunch of inebriated, emotionally flattened nitwits. Their crystals and their wind chimes, their mandalas and meaningless exhortations to be self-aware while they spend their whole lives talking – endlessly! They're posers. They don't know shit.

'I don't know anything,' she says. 'It's taken me all this time, to get right to the end to fully appreciate that.'

This admission silences me and I try to remind myself of the nasty woman who checked into the Samarang a few weeks back: the pompous contempt with which she regarded me; the way she'd suggested that Bill Carstens, my predecessor, ran the hotel better than I did; the way she stood with frumpish indignation waiting for Sith to open the doors.

What I need from Nancy is a clear and unshakeable idea of her – a definition, as unambiguous as her very own name – that will properly describe what kind of person she is; who she is here and now and in perpetuity. And if I'm unable to grasp that, then she will forever remain an unpredictable and inscrutable character – which is precisely how I regard the rest of the human race (of which I have a very dim view).

I can't be sure if I like Nancy or despise her.

10

There are tiny villages built on the hillsides. Mostly, brick and wood. Some have thatched roofs. They have cooking spaces outside and a communal water pump where the women wash themselves fully covered in bright cotton gowns. Chickens strut about. Puppies gambol in the doorways. Pigs slouch in the shade. Corn cobs dry in the sun. Kids with no pants totter after their mothers. These places remind me of the villages in Africa. It's the same old world.

At these altitudes the hills are less forested. Grassy slopes dotted with alpine trees, fold into lush tropical crevices. This is where they used to grow opium. I'm mindful of this. People and their oblivion. Not knowing.

As we near Phou Nang Fa, Nancy tells me more of her story.

After leaving the capital in the middle of the night back in 1975, being plucked from her father's embrace at the airport for one last time, she and her mother and brother boarded a flight for Hong Kong and then another to Paris. There they lived until Nancy was 18. She speaks fluent French. And Swedish and English and even bit of the Khmu language that they speak in these hills. People who speak many languages annoy me.

Her mother was courted by a French filmmaker who produced a documentary about her. It was a story of struggle and ardour and the triumph of the human spirit over tyranny. The mother was much admired by the artsy types of Paris, but she did not appreciate that kind of attention. So they bumbled about for a few years, moving to Geneva and then to Stockholm and then to London.

Her brother took a job with the UN in New York. He was fired after standing up in a meeting and yelling all kinds of profanities at the secretary general, Perez de Cuellar.

'Perez de Cuellar? I remember him.'

'He couldn't stand the man. Couldn't stand the UN. He said it was a club for the white man and the white man's black. There was a thing in the papers. My brother moved to Missouri. He married and had seven children. He wrote a book, advocating the revival of the Non-Aligned Movement. Not exactly a bestseller. He worked as a lecturer at a technical college. Now he has Alzheimer's and can't even remember his own name.'

'Oh no.'

A club for the white man and the white man's black? It sounds ludicrous to me, but I laugh at the thought of it.

Nancy explains: 'My brother always argued that the UN was set up when the entire continent of Africa – just about – was represented by Western powers, much of Asia too. Not to mention the Americas: the natives overrun by the mother tongues of Europe. But no matter your mother tongue, we were all corralled into it. It was part of the package. It had all the trappings of an exclusive gentlemen's club where the founding members, who'd just decided to take their foot off your neck, were now inviting you inside, imploring you to observe what they liked to call an *international standard.* It was a white man's game. My brother became offended by the whole idea of it. Enraged, really. Corrupt dictators with their kaftans and fly-whisks and fezzes all courted into the sanctum of the General Assembly – colourful, yes, in a sort of cute, global village kind of way, but utterly powerless too. It was a fraud. So he left and retired, derided, in obscurity.'

I feel that I am warming to Nancy (or at least to her brother). I've always resented UN types – especially in this country. They cruise around in their white trucks with their laptops and their upliftment programs coaxing the people of the world into a state of brittle fragmentation, with each fragmented part connected to each other part by a brittle set of rules. Refugees piling up at border gates. The UN sends them tents. They're a supercilious lot – those UN types.

Nancy continues: 'I suppose in a personal sort of way I rather agree with him, my brother. Half of me is from Pho Daeng and the other half from Stockholm. Lived in Paris, in London and then in Fort Lauderdale. Carry a British passport.'

'Ha!' I say. 'Just like me! A colonial orphan!'

She grunts, a little amused. 'I suppose we're all colonial orphans in a way – loyal to these constructs, these nations; aspiring to live on a static flat space – a map – sliced into neat equidistant parallel lines of longitude and latitude, all of us permanently enjoying our own fixed plot. But it's a tragic delusion. There are no plots here. Instead we're clinging to a cannonball that spins, wobbles and hurtles around a giant ball of flame, giving us night and day, the seasons and all their unpredictable consequences. The earth. We can't stand it, wish the damn thing would stop.'

This is all rather a lot to comprehend. True, I don't really like the earth either if I'm to be honest. Yes, there is scenery – such as the scenery through which we are now travelling – that is appealing, but hidden out there are all kinds of pernicious threats and perfectly deadly possibilities. It's no wonder we travel through it in a huge, gas powered, air-conditioned, high-speed machine made of reflective aluminium panels, crammed with life-saving airbags; enjoying the view through sealed windows of thickened glass at a quickened pace in complete silence. It might well be that none of us really likes the earth as we drive all over it in these defiant machines.

And yes, there are other things like food which is tasty (and all of which is potentially poisonous), sex which is titillating (and which spawns disease, shame and betrayal) and comedy (which is invariably born out of some kind of unspeakable malice). And there is of course booze (which destroys the liver and has everyone around you crying over your folly). So no, in all, not a pretty picture. I don't make any of these admissions to Nancy. Normally I would. I'd be ranting. But right now, I just don't feel like it.

After another long silence I say, 'Fort Lauderdale?'

'That's where Bacon comes from. I married a man called Bacon. It only lasted five years. It surprises me that I've still kept the name. I suppose in a funny sort of way it adds to my mystique!' She grunts again.

'He was American?'

'English. Worked as an agent for sporting icons.'

'Sounds horrendous.'

'It was.'

'And you? What were you? Did you work?'

'I taught swimming. I worked as a swimming teacher at a high school.' But I can tell she doesn't really want to talk about those days. 'Look!' she says with some relief. 'Look, over there, to the right. Do you see it? That's Phou Nang Fa. The mountain.'

Beyond the rippling pattern of bluish hills there is a mountain that stands proudly amongst them. She leans graciously towards the east, has a rounded sloping hump that fades towards the west. Her face is firm and steep. The first thing I think of is Mother Earth. The same earth I despise. I think of Mother Nature. I think of the Mother Continent.

It is nearly dark when we arrive in Nancy's ancestral town of Pho Daeng.

That night I have a dream. My daughter, Angela, is standing on a low stone wall next to the sea. Her son, Marcus, a dark-haired, gangly kid of about nine, is walking along the top of the wall his arms out on either side of him, as if in the midst of a careful balancing act. He says to Angela, 'Look, look up there!' He's pointing up to Table Mountain. There they are in Cape Town – those two – in a place we like to call the Mother City. And Angela says, 'I know. I know. It's called Phou Nang Fa.' I'm standing somewhere over the sea – this massive churning body of saltwater. I see little pieces of excrement floating on the surface. And I'm screaming at her; at them: 'It's not called Phou Nang Fa! It's not! It's not!' But the wind whips these feeble words from my mouth and crushes them in the storm, never to be heard.

I wake up with a start. I knock over the quarter full bottle of Scotch. I'm incredibly thirsty.

In the morning we take a good look around the town of Pho Daeng. We are checked in to the not-very-imaginatively-named Mountain View Guesthouse – a small, dilapidated shophouse with grubby walls, leaking pipes and a restaurant at street level with plastic chairs and steel tables. I grimace. It is owned by a slovenly, po-faced Chinese woman who seems put out at our arrival. But still in all its flaws I do get the feeling that this is a curious adventure – one of which I am proud. I almost feel like taking a selfie, even asking Wai Ming to make a video of me as I walk along the quiet single street of the village, high in the mountains, as if I'm David Attenborough at the furthest ends of the earth on a noble quest to find a rare, poisonous androgynous arachnid. I fancy myself as a great explorer out here in the mountainous regions of Laos.

But I don't take a selfie or a video. I stopped doing that a long time ago. I had few people to send those records to and even of the few on my list, none were really that interested.

We had – the three of us – breakfasted in the restaurant. Noodle soup with herbs and glutinous lumps of ... something, stuck to softened bone. It was surprisingly edible. Now Wai Ming and I are walking up the road while Nancy stays in her room, sitting in her chair, staring out of a small window at the mountain of Phou Nang Fa.

The houses are all built close to the edge of this main thoroughfare. They have wooden shutters and their doors open directly onto the street. Some of the buildings are not plastered, built of cement blocks, while others are painted in vivid colours – pinks, purples, greens. A group of school children in haphazard blue and white uniforms – some trundle wearily, some skip merrily – are on their way to school. A woman squats in a doorway, before a large aluminium sink, washing plastic plates. A shirtless man with a wizened face and a smooth belly is standing on a roof. He glances at us briefly and then settles on his haunches and begins smiting his hammer, nailing down a piece of iron onto a truss. Another woman sits at a window. She is old with an intricately wrinkled face, narrow eyes and sunken cheeks. She looks at us disconsolately as if we are harmless phantoms.

In between the gaps of these dwellings, I catch glimpses of the steep valleys below. The town, so I discern, is built on a narrow crest. To the west, the hills and gullies through which we travelled yesterday and to the east, the giant motherly formation of Phou Nang Fa itself.

Nancy has promised that we will drive to the foot of Phou Nang Fa later in the day. I am looking forward to it in a way that I haven't looked forward to something since I was a kid – a funfair, a movie, a trip to a waterfall, Christmas.

For now she is in her room, soused on morphine, meditating. This is what she tells me.

'There is no temple in this town,' Wai Ming remarks.

'Really? That's amazing. I though they all had temples.'

'Not this one. They practice what everyone likes to call animism.'

'Oh yes, I've heard of that.'

'God will build his temple in the heart, on the ruins of churches and religions. That was Emerson. He wasn't sure about the bricks and mortar cathedrals or even the so-called holy books.

They obstruct what is really important about a religious idea. It concerned him that the symbol had become synonymous with that which it symbolized. At that point symbolism – metaphor if you like – loses its power. This is what has troubled me most of my life. I was born and raised a Catholic you see.'

'Ah, Catholic,' I say. They seem such a troubled lot, those Catholics. They're always telling people how they were born and raised in the faith. They're always telling people about their guilt. I'm glad I'm not a Catholic. Presbyterian me. Easy. A few sing-songs at Sunday School. Nothing more. Catholics always seem to be so depressed about being Catholics. Aside from this I'm not sure I understand much of what Wai Ming is telling me. This isn't my kind of conversation. 'Not easy being Catholic,' I say.

He glances at me curiously.

'I mean, as far as I can tell,' I add unhelpfully.

We walk along the road and I feel inadequate. I'd like to think Wai Ming is a bit smug; a bit intellectual, but I can't be sure of that. I even feel slightly guilty for thinking that about him. So my thoughts lurch again towards that quarter bottle of Scotch in my room.

Wai Ming doesn't say another thing. Perhaps he can sense that I'm not really interested in religious mumbo-jumbo. I am a simpler kind of man. I like my good times. I like my booze and my smokes, my jokes and my girls. I can't understand why the hell it's all so complicated, but these are the things I like and I think I should have more of them.

We walk to the end of the village. The air is unexpectedly chilly. I look out at Phou Nang Fa and I am strangely quieted by her perfect shape – it is markedly asymmetrical and yet she has a pleasing curve to her spine and a reassuring sharpness to her face. A huge lorry comes tearing down the main strip. It thunders past us. A whirlwind of grit and dust is aroused in its spirited wake. I cover my mouth and close my eyes. 'Fucker,' I say.

Wai Ming laughs.

We turn and begin walking down the road back into the village. A very small old woman with an emphatically hunched spine appears from a discreet path that leads down between two houses and into the steep valley beyond. Her head hangs irresistibly towards the ground, as if she's searching, with fading eyesight, for a final resting place. She has lived on these hillsides her whole life, hunched forward, tilling these steep fields. Now she is unmistakeably near the end.

I say, 'My God, look at that old thing. One wonders how she keeps going.'

'*Why* she keeps going is an even better question.'

'Exactly. Why?'

After a short pause, Wai Ming says, 'Well, I suppose she's got to see how the story ends.'

You've got to see how the story ends. I've heard that before. It's a statement that antagonizes and impresses me at the same time.

I'll say it again: I'm a simple man. And I don't understand why it's all so complicated. I feel as if I want to be sick.

The people in Laos, many of them have little spirit houses outside their dwellings. These are miniature temples, quite lavishly decorated some of them. Folks have popped meagre offerings at the tiny doors of the spirit houses: a bunch of bananas, a mango, a bottle of fizzy drink, marigolds, candles, joss-sticks, small figurines covered in glitter. Some of them are even festooned with little twinkly lights, of exactly the same kind that we'd put on a Christmas tree. There are few such spirit houses in the town of Pho Daeng, but I spot one, a rather drab one, outside a small shop with its shutters drawn.

'They look kind of cute, those little mini-houses,' I say and then I immediately regret this comment because I suspect that Wai Ming is going to tell me about some mystical 'spirit concept' that makes no sense.

'They're intended to be cute; to entice the evil spirits. They will tell you that evil is not here to be banished. It is here to courted, to form the fullness of each story. In the same way that shadow fulfils the story of light.'

There he goes again.

'I see,' I say. But I don't see. Still I ponder his remarks as we amble back to the Mountain View Guesthouse. 'But you're supposed to be Singaporean, one of the most sophisticated, civilized nations on earth. I mean, you can't go around believing in all this hocus-pocus.'

For the first time Wai Ming laughs out loud. 'Singaporeans are obsessed with this stuff. More than ever!' he laughs again. 'And so we should be. We've abandoned the kind of self-awareness that these symbols inspire. So we perform the rituals more incessantly than ever, praying for more and more good fortune knowing that it is less and less deserved. We're in a bit of panic down there, in Singapore.'

I nod my head. But I'm in firm disagreement with him. I've been to Singapore myself. Frankly, he has no idea what he's talking about. It's the most organised, functional country in the world. It's what we're all after! A taxi driver who was ferrying me to Changi airport once said to me, 'You know what the problem with Singapore is? It's that we've got nothing to complain about. Everyone around the world likes to sit in bars and complain. But in Singapore we sit in bars and stare at our phones because we've got nothing to say!' He laughed, that taxi driver. He laughed until he had tears in his eyes. I suppose it's what passes for Singaporean humour. But still, he was right. They've got nothing to complain about. What the hell is Wai Ming telling me about them all being in a panic?

I recount my story about the taxi driver to Wai Ming.

Wai Ming grunts and says, 'You say he had tears in his eyes?'

'Yes.'

'Huh. I bet he did.'

We return to the guesthouse and the po-faced Chinese owner seems to have befriended Nancy. She sits in a plastic chair, stripping the leaves off stalks of basil and tossing them into a plastic bowl. Nancy sits opposite her in her wheelchair. She has a rug over her lap and wears a thick jacket. Although I do not hear them speak, it seems as if we have interrupted a conversation.

The Chinese woman glances at me sourly and then resumes with her leaf plucking as if I'm not in the room.

'Good walk?' Nancy says.

'Oh yes. Nice. Nice and cool up here. And old Wai Ming's been prattling on about the spirit world and how depressing it is to be Catholic.'

I grin at him mischievously but Nancy looks at me indignantly. 'I should hardly think he was prattling.'

'Well, you know, I mean he does *go on*. Spirits and rituals and energy treatments and superstitions. It's all a bit, you know, *out there*!'

But they are not amused. 'You mean none of it is to be believed?'

'Oh I should think so. Let's face it, you know, we have evolved over the last few millennia, after all. We used to think that lightning was a warning from God but now we've worked out that it's simply caused by the earth and the sun and the friction and so on … The point is, you can believe what you want but the facts are the facts, I'm afraid.'

I feel tension emerge between us and even the Chinese lady looks up at me and senses that I'm a misfit here; should keep my mouth shut.

Nancy looks at me severely. 'Do you know the facts or do you just perceive them? Quite frankly, it doesn't sound as if you're terribly sure about what lightning is at all. So few of us really do. Does that mean that so few of us know the truth? Or is the truth just for them, the ones that went out into the storm with their instruments and barometers and came up with a plausible theory? Do we just take their word for it? Or is the truth something else entirely? Something universally available to us? Isn't it just about the way we feel – the way we feel from one moment to the next, entirely inexplicable, but still … so real?'

'I have no idea what you're talking about Nancy and yes, in

any case, I think we should trust the people that go out into the storm with their measuring devices. They're scientists. They've worked it out. If the truth is just something you feel why is it that we're longer afraid of lightning?

'Aren't we?'

There is a brisk pause.

'Well, not in that way. Not in that sort of, oh-my-God-he's-coming-to-punish-us kind of way.'

'Really? For my part, lightning provokes and inspires me in profound ways, far more profoundly than knowing how or why it happens. You try sitting in this chair. Doing what I'm doing. Then you might not be so sure about the supremacy of the facts.'

Now there is a very long pause.

Eventually I say, 'I'm going to my room'.

I take a drop of whisky. I lie on my bed and stare at a damp pock-marked ceiling. I *am* doing what Nancy's doing. I've been doing it all my life. I might not be in that chair … yet. But I'm on precisely the same trajectory.

I finish the whisky and I feel angry. That's what I feel. That's the truth.

At around midday Wai Ming knocks gently at my door. 'Hi Julian. Nancy says we're ready to go to the mountain. You up for it?'

'I ummm, yes. Sure. I'll be down in a minute.' I am unsteady on my feet as I walk downstairs. Nancy is in her chair with a heightened look of expectation on her face. But when she sees me her expression falters.

'You've been drinking.'

'I ... uhhh ... well a bit.'

'I thought we agreed no drinking and driving.'

'I'm fine!' I rail. 'Fine, fine, fine!'

Nancy lets out a long sigh. I barrel towards the car, fetching the keys from my pocket. 'Come on! Let's go to the mountain!' I know I sound a little scathing; a little bit deranged.

'No. No not today. We'll have to go tomorrow.' She turns and wheels herself to her room.

Wai Ming shrugs his shoulders – impossible to discern what he means by that – and he follows her.

11

I'm hungry. So I sit in the restaurant and eat another bowl of noodle soup – the same thing I had for breakfast. There is a fridge near the door and I help myself to a few cans of beer. There is a TV against the wall, and I flick through the channels in hurried agitation. They're all Asian – the channels. Singing contests, military parades and soap operas featuring ancestral ghosts. I think I'm going out of my mind, stuck out here in this mountain village.

The Chinese woman has slightly blackened teeth and she sits at a table in the dim recesses of the restaurant. She too is eating noodles. Sometimes she looks up from her bowl and it seems as if she is scowling at me. It's obvious that she truly hates me. The noodles seem to quiver in terror as she sucks them into her mouth. She chews her food with a mincing side-winding movement of her gums, turning her food into cud. It's the first time I've ever felt sorry for a noodle.

I return to my room and lie on my bed. It's cold. I wrap a blanket around me and try to sleep. And within a few minutes I'm back on my feet, heading for the little shop near the entrance to the town. It's a wooden building that leans precariously to one side. But they do have an impressive selection of booze – even if it's nothing I recognize. I don't recognize the cigarette brands either. I inspect the display with the keenness of a connoisseur and eventually select a bottle only because it has a bit of English on the label. Big Luck Golden Whisky! I take a closer look. They've misspelt whisky! It's 'Whiksy'! I want to laugh out loud. I see a symbol that I recognise: 43%. That'll do. And it seems to be the right colour. Certainly has that smoky golden hue. I buy two boxes of unrecognizable cigarettes and march back to my room.

That night there is a storm. The wind pounds the fragile village – these tiny buildings on a narrow crest – and it feels as if the whole town will soon be plucked from its roots, lifted into the air and hurled into a valley while rain and lightning bang about us. So much for courting the evil spirits! I laugh.

In the morning I have a cracking headache and a runny tummy. It is late when I emerge and Nancy and Wai Ming are sitting in the restaurant. They look at me with undisguised consternation.

'We can't go to Phou Nang Fa today either,' she says flatly. 'The rains last night have blocked the road apparently. We'll have to wait for the rivers to subside a bit. They've burst their banks.'

'I see.'

'Some noodle soup?' Wai Ming says. Wai Ming likes to keep things light; keep things moving on.

'Sure.'

But I don't want noodle soup. I want bacon and eggs, sausages, beans and toast. Noodle soup! Give me a goddamn break!

'So, we are stuck here in Pho Daeng for another day,' I say glumly.

Nancy and Wai Ming both nod and look out the front of the shop. They're not in a conversational mood it seems.

The Chinese lady places a bowl of soup before me. I see

glutinous lumps of meat and little pools of oil floating on the surface. No. I can't. I run to my room to be sick.

A short while later, I'm lying on my bed. Tears leak from the corners of my eyes and I feel pain swelling in my bloodshot head. I lie on my back and breathe and I recognize this as a low point. It's another one of those low points. Fuck!

There is a knock at my door and I hear Wai Ming say, 'Hey, Julian. Can you open the door?'

'Of course!' I stumble to the door.

He smiles at me with his usual warmth – the saintly little prick – and says, 'I've got you some aspirin. Have you thrown up? It looked as if you needed to throw up.'

'I've thrown up all right.'

'Good. That's a good sign.'

'Oh it is, is it?'

I swallow the two aspirin. 'Thanks.'

I lie back on my bed and pull the blanket over me with flustered agitation. I know I want to cry again but Wai Ming is in the room and I'm not going to do it. Not!

I begin to sob.

'You're in pain?'

'I've got a cracking fucking headache.'

'Here,' he says. 'Lie back. You're okay.'

I face the ceiling and I sense that he is squatting near the end of my bed. He then takes hold of my feet, my ankles, and holds them in his hands. I'm embarrassed by this. My feet are in poor shape. Bloated. Speckled with red blotches. The toenails are brittle and grey, the colour of concrete. The skin on the heel is cracked, sometimes bleeding. No one ever looks at my hideous feet. Not even me.

'Be still,' he says.

I am still. Strangely so. The urge to cry slowly dissipates. I just lie there and breathe while a Singaporean palliative care specialist who's in a self-confessed panic holds my feet administering some kind of energy treatment.

'The thing is,' I say. I am feeling mightily ashamed. 'I've been under a lot of pressure at work. You know. We had a dead Russian. You can't trust those fucking Russians. He was some kind of agent. They think I stole something from his room. The Russians are after me. MI5 is after me. Mossad is probably after me. And I'm just a low-life hotel manager. I've been placed on suspension. They'll probably kill me, shove my corpse into the trunk of an old Mercedes.'

'Shhh,' Wai Ming says. He is still holding my feet and I hear the sound of rain falling.

When I wake up it is dark. The bottle of Big Luck Golden Whiksy is empty. I am unusually calm.

I drift in and out of dreams. I'm standing on a hillside in Africa – somewhere in my old Rhodesia. I am surrounded by other men, I don't recognize any of them but I know them to be friends. They're all quite old. They are my father's friends. We're drinking beer and admiring the sunset while swathes of animals move in great herds across the valley – elephants and wildebeest and a few elegant giraffes. We're all quaffing our beers and laughing and backslapping and then I realize that my beer tastes off. It utterly disgusts me. I don't say anything. I take another one off the table and it's off too. I take another and another and they're all bad, distinctively syrupy and lumpy. None of the other men seem to notice and I don't say anything. I laugh along with them. I laugh weakly.

And then I am back in this room at the guesthouse. I can't tell if this is part of a dream. Maureen appears at the door and walks towards my bed. Well, it *looks* like Maureen, but it's not her. It's my mother. And she says, 'I'm quite all right, you know, Jules. I'm quite okay.' She was the only person who ever called me Jules and didn't think it was weird.

'Mum!' I cry.

She looks at me sternly and says, 'Where is Angela? I thought she'd be here. What have you done? Why isn't Angela here?' My mother is still calm, but distinctively sad.

'She's at home. She's with Marcus. She's … she's living near the mountain.'

'Ah, the mountain. You tell her I came. Tell her.'

On our third day the rivers have subsided and I am sober. So, we're all set. We finally commence our journey to the foot of Phou Nang Fa.

Nancy, Wai Ming and I have breakfasted – yes, noodle soup – and we have reunited in a spirit of amity and surprising congeniality. I drive with deliberate caution, keep my mouth shut, hoping to keep our delicate peace intact. We travel along a narrow dirt road, carved out of the sides of steep slopes. The bends are tight and the track is submerged here and there by orange muddy pools. I engage the diff lock and the car rumbles through them while mud spatters the windows. I feel inestimably proud of myself; my skills as an off-road driver. I feel safe, pristinely untouched by nature, in the cabin of this car; ensconced in this silent bubble of polymers and plastics, powered by a fuel combustion engine. We reach the bottom of a valley, cross over a river and commence our ascent up the next slope.

Nancy is positively chipper. I almost forget that she has only weeks to live. 'Oh it's so lush. Each leaf is dripping wet. And the rivers are all thundering through the valleys! White clouds aloft!' She winds down the window. 'And that musty smell of decay!' She seems almost ecstatic.

I feel like saying something scornful; to berate her for celebrating the musty smell of decay, but somehow, I know what she means and I say, 'Oh yes, it's great.'

We stop at the top of the next slope. Nancy needs morphine. I sense that these stops are becoming more frequent.

I stand outside the vehicle, smoking. The cicadas are shrill. I can't quite decide if it's the sound of celebration or the sound of alarm. Frogs squawk with sullen laziness, disguising their sensual intent. Spiders silently spin their webs, making their homes, their traps. Teeming with life one might say, and still there is that musty smell of decay. It all seems unstoppable. The decay and the life.

This reminds me of an Indian I once knew in Durban. He was a barman at the Azure Waters Hotel – the one from which I was fired. He told me about a concept called creative destruction. He was annoyed because he'd seen an American on TV who had said that this was an American concept which supported market dynamics. He was clearly irate.

'And why does that annoy you?' I'd said.

'Because it's not an American concept. It's ancient! This is Shiva. The God of Destruction!'

I've never forgotten that. I've often found myself pondering the idea: a God of Destruction! What an absurd thing!

Those Indians!

When we're back in the car and descending once more into a valley, I decide to offer Nancy and Wai Ming a bit of my worldly grasp of Hindu philosophy. 'You know I had a friend once, in Durban,' I say. 'He was a Hindu. He taught me all about Shiva, the God of Destruction. Can you believe that? Those Hindus have a God of Destruction!'

Nancy smiles at me and turns her head to face Wai Ming in the back seat, but she is unable to turn fully. She is in a bit of pain and returns to face the front.

Wai Ming says, 'What made you think of that?'

'It's all the bugs. The bugs and spiders and so on outside. They're all alive out there. They're doing their thing, making their bleeping noises and spinning their webs. They're doing all this in the midst of this unmistakeable smell of decay. They don't seem to notice. Or if they do, it doesn't seem to matter. It's as if they're a part of it. They don't give up.'

Wai Ming laughs out loud. It's an odd girlish sound. I almost feel a bit sorry for him – having a laugh like that. 'I think you're right,' he says. 'That is perhaps what Shiva represents. The decay.' He seems quite suddenly animated. 'You know the Chinese have an ancient saying: midday, for all the light about, is when midnight is born.'

'That's not a Chinese saying! That's U2! Remember? How

did it go?' I try to remember the lyrics to that U2 song from the 90s. What was it? Something about midnight. Then it hits me! 'Midnight is when the day begins!' I'm almost euphoric. I start singing it. 'Midniii-iii-iii-ght is when the day begins ... der der der di der ...'

Wai Ming laughs a bit sheepishly and says, 'Well, that's a little bit different from the Chinese. It has a different emphasis. The Chinese are describing the birth of midnight. Your Irish friends are describing the birth of day.'

'It's the same thing! It's a cycle!'

'It's a cycle all right. But we are looking at different sides of it. One expresses hope for the day. The other expresses acceptance of the night. It's a bit of a different attitude.'

For a moment I thought that I might have outsmarted Wai Ming with a little contemporary wisdom of my own (even if it was from the 90s, still, it was decidedly more contemporary than an ancient Chinese saying). But no, I hadn't. Again, I'd like to say that he's a pompous little fellow, but somehow that feels unfair. He makes me feel like a bozo, that's true, but I can't accuse him of being pompous. He is, in all fairness, a gentle soul.

Nancy says, 'You've been dreaming, haven't you?'

I suddenly feel myself sweating. She looks at me with her familiar formidable firmness.

'Dreaming? Yes. I have actually. What? What do you mean by that?'

She smiles again and looks ahead. 'I don't mean anything by it. I was just asking.' She still has that smile on her face.

We traverse another river. The water is still high after the rains and it runs over a concrete weir. This journey is much longer than I thought it would be.

After another long silence, Nancy turns to me again and says, 'Do you know if you've ever loved?'

'Loved?'

She nods calmly.

'Of course, I've loved. I was married once. I've already told you!'

'That's not what I mean. I mean, have you ever loved something so much that you have accepted it fully? Isn't that what they say in the vow? For better or worse?'

I'm having trouble with this question, because Maureen and I are now divorced. I've told Nancy that we settled amicably, but we didn't. I couldn't bear the woman. Can't say I ever loved her for *worse*. I loved her for *better*, when she was still raunchy and voluptuous. As soon as she no longer seduced me the way other women did, I couldn't wait to get rid of her quite frankly. She was a trap. That's what it felt like. A trap.

'I don't know,' I say at last.

'It's all right,' she says. 'You'll find out. You want to find out. I can tell. The truth is there. It's hidden, protected by symbols. The symbols of your dreams. The symbols of this forest. You can let go of the facts, Julian, and follow the symbols.'

I am oddly comforted by these words. This is perhaps the first thing that Nancy has said to me that has actually made me a feel a little bit better. I'm grateful to her and I say, 'Thanks.'

'We're nearly there,' Nancy says. 'I can feel it.'

Nancy is right. Around the next bend, there she is. Phou

Nang Fa, the great Mother Mountain. Her face; her jagged walls soar above us, marked with inky tears. I feel her observing us, unmoved, even unimpressed as we bounce along the muddy track in our tiny car. She carries with her an expression of sadness, of inestimable loss, of immutable power. I suddenly feel reduced to a blithering panic and focus on the road ahead, the quivering dials on the dashboard, with a sort of stubborn bloody-mindedness, unable to look up and face the old Mother Mountain.

There is a flat space, a floor of rounded pebbles, near a stream and we pull up.

I get out of the car and look at the stream. I have an inexplicable urge to rip off all my clothes and jump into the water, submerge myself in it. But I don't. I walk around the other side and help Wai Ming carry Nancy from the car into the wheelchair.

The ground is too uneven and bumpy for the wheelchair to move across it so Wai Ming and I lift it up – with Nancy sitting in it – and we carry it to the water's edge.

'It's in the shade,' Wai Ming observes.

'In the shadow,' Nancy says with her usual dry laugh.

We stand back. In the shadow of this great ancient formation, us three flummoxed pulsating beings, dither a bit this way and that – not sure what to do next.

'You've been the perfect gentlemen,' Nancy says.

'Ha, I haven't been called that in a long time … not unless someone was paying me for it,' I say.

Nancy smiles gently. 'Now leave me here for a little bit. I don't know how long I'll be, but you must leave me alone for a bit.'

'We'll walk downstream,' Wai Ming says.

'That'll be fine.' Nancy faces the rock walls of the mountain. I can't tell if she is at all apprehensive, but there seems to be a certain stiffness to her posture.

Wai Ming and I step away and with a strange sort of meekness we retreat, heading downstream.

We take our seats on a rock that juts out over the stream. We still have sight of Nancy in her chair, but we are out of earshot and leave her in silence – except that it's not silence. There remain the gushing, gurgling noises of the water and the whirring, bleeping, ticking cacophony of the forest. But still, it feels like silence.

'What exactly is this?' I say to Wai Ming.

'Remember how Nancy said that this is where she takes comfort in her mortality? She has travelled all over the world and no place does this to her quite as much as Phou Nang Fa.'

We sit in silence for some time. I smoke. I flick the butts into the stream. 'I don't get it,' I say finally. 'I don't get this thing you're on. Both of you. She's about to die. I mean, that's …' I look up and see the small dying woman, hunched in her special chair. She wears a light-blue cardigan around her shoulders. Her hair is just a deadening kind of grey. I know that I don't want Nancy to die. I can't bear it. It's terrible.

'It's terrible,' I say at last.

'I know,' Wai Ming says. 'It *is* terrible. But there's a way of doing it; dying, that is. That's what we're all trying to figure out. It's all we're ever trying to figure out. No one really likes the idea of it.'

'Sometimes I do. Sometimes I think I could go in the next heartbeat and I'd be nothing but relieved.'

'I think we all feel that from time to time. That's true.'

The earth moves on its arc and the shadows slip away, sliding ever further into the crevices, in search of refuge from that infernal light and then slowly, almost surreptitiously they creep out and being to expand on the eastern edges of the mountain.

I think of shadow and light. Conventional wisdom beseeches us to find the light.

'Funny,' I say. 'I was just thinking. Pure light will leave us just as blind as pure darkness.'

Wai Ming looks at me intently. 'That's excellent,' he says. 'I really, really ... love that.'

He smiles broadly at me and I smile back at him. I feel proud of myself and wonder if there's anything else in me that might impress him. Somehow, despite the possibility that I might be teetering on the cusp of yet another epiphany, I am compelled to stay silent.

The sunlight has almost reached Nancy who sits still, immobile in her chair on the pebble river bed. 'I'll go and check on her. Best she avoids too much sun.'

With Wai Ming strolling away I look again at the stream. Dots of light dance on its surface. I am reminded of my earlier urge to strip off and immerse myself in the water. I look up and see Wai Ming squatting on his haunches beside the wheelchair. That image almost makes me want to cry. These two tiny beings in the shadows of the earth, comforting each other. I see him stand and walk to the car. She needs more morphine.

When Wai Ming returns, he says, 'She wants to stay a bit longer.'

He has brought her a broad sun hat and she sits there, still immobile, while the sunlight sparkles on the brim of her hat.

'What does she mean that I should forget about the facts and follow the symbols? What does she mean when she says that the truth is protected by symbols. Protected from what?'

'From us!' Wai Ming replies. 'Somehow we have it in our heads that the truth is something we get to reject; to outwit. So, the truth is protected by the symbols; protected from rejection. They guide you to towards an understanding of what your life really is. If it was all literal, if our dreams were literal, if life were presented to us in a literal way, we would deny it, we would reject it. So the symbols conceal the truth as much as they guide us towards it; prevent us from crushing it with our usual painstaking rationality.'

'I've got a friend back in town. We drink together. He's a writer. He told me that the water image is very powerful. And it's a bit strange really because Nancy and I were at that ceremony for the dead Russian a few weeks back. And while I was there I had this vision of a river. I suppose that's the sort of thing you're talking about.'

'I guess it is. Your friend is right. Water images are powerful. They're very common too. Most of us ignore this kind of thing. We wait for science – its weary plod through the centuries – to reveal it to us in a literal way. We refuse to grant the image any meaning, living and dying in the most appalling, self-inflicted angst.'

'And she's a swimming teacher,' I say. 'The water image again.'

'Precisely.'

I've run out of cigarettes and feel agitated that I've forgotten to bring an extra pack. I look up at Phou Nang Fa. Maybe she isn't sad after all. I can't make it out. Her face – her countenance – as brittle as it may be, seems to shift and vary; grimace and grin; weep and laugh.

We have been here for nearly three hours. This surprises me when I look at my watch. I'm feeling a bit hungry.

'You hungry?' Wai Ming says.

I'm amused by his question; its perfect timing. 'Yes. A bit. Do you think we should be getting back?'

We return to Nancy. She is so still I wonder, for a brief horrifying moment, if she might have died. But when we stand before her, she looks up to face us, squinting in the light. Tears are drying on her cheeks.

'Are we leaving now?'

'Yes, Nancy. It's a long way back. We must get you home.'

She looks back at the stream. 'I'm ready to go.'

We carry her – wheelchair and all – back to the car. We buckle her into the front seat. Wai Ming jumps into the back seat. Just as I am about to climb into the driver's seat I stop. No. I can't go. Not yet.

'I'm sorry,' I say and I begin running to the water's edge. I don't want to have to explain myself. It's too complicated; not properly comprehended – even by me. The shadows are growing long again and I remove my shirt. I know this is an unpleasant thing for them to look at. It's outrageous. I run along the pebbles, further away. There is a tuft of tall reeds on the river bank and I slip behind them. I remove everything. My clothes, my watch, even a brass bangle that I wear on my wrist. The lot. I'm supremely naked and I jump into the river. It's icy. I lie flat on the rounded, mossy rocks and let the water flow right over my body. My veins crackle at the shock of it. I keep my head down, holding my breath, and let the force of the water strike the crown of my lowered head, pummel my pale, flabby limbs, drain me of energy; revive me while I cling helplessly to a rock – a large round dead stone – embedded in the earth, in the middle of this shaded river.

12

We pull up beneath the main portico of the Samarang. The portico is a fiercely geometric construction, like a Chinese fan, its edges sharp and triangular. It looms forward over the driveway in an expression that is slightly prickly, almost hostile. I've not seen the hotel in this way before.

The car is suitably speckled with mud, with large dry cakes of it under the mudguards. I like the look. It is obvious that we have been on an exotic adventure in the jungle and I hope anyone who sees us is pointedly jealous.

On the journey, Nancy had explained that she had known about her illness for more than a year. She had declined chemotherapy or any other kind of therapy and would allow the mutational aberration to do what it must. Yes, she had a daughter once, a little thing called Mary, who died in a drowning accident when she was six. What added to the ordeal was not only that Nancy was her mother, but she was her swimming teacher too. For all her quiet contemplation of mortality, it seemed to me that she'd never quite forgiven herself for the manner or circumstances of Mary's death. 'The pain is real,' she had said. 'It's always very real.'

Her husband had remarried multiple times and for all she could discern from their infrequent contact, was that he was living in Costa Rica with a 22-year-old Slovenian girl.

Her brother, of course, still survived: the one in America, with Alzheimer's and seven children. A niece or two had popped in to see her just before she left London.

Now, all that was left Nancy was the company of Wai Ming and me.

And do you know that when we left the foot of Phou Nang Fa and drove along the muddy track back to Pho Daeng village on the crest – a journey of more than three hours – none of us said a word, not a single word for the entire time? I have to mention that. I'm amazed by that.

Sith and his helpers open the doors of the car with alacrity. They smile broadly and welcome us with genuine delight. I am comforted by their presence, my Lao team, and am suddenly aware of my affection for them – something I'd not appreciated before. When I'd first arrived in Laos I used to call them the Samarang Gang and they all loved it. Then Jacques joined us and I stopped saying it. Now, we enter the lobby of the hotel and, apart from the friendship of the Samarang Gang, the setting seems strangely unfamiliar to me – as if it was a long time since I was last here; decades.

Nancy is in her wheelchair. I lean forward and put my arms around her neck. 'Thank you. It's been a journey.'

She puts her arms around my neck too and presses her forehead against mine. 'Thank you. I'm so glad you were the one.'

I'm not sure what to make of this remark.

I watch Wai Ming push the wheelchair towards the elevators, followed by Sith who pushes the bellman's trolley. I am about to turn and leave the hotel when Jacques comes bounding towards me from the Frangipani Room.

'Hey, Julian!'

'Hello, Jacques.'

'How did it all go?'

'Fine, fine. You know ... fine.'

'Oh great. You were gone longer than expected. Couldn't be sure how to find you if you just ... disappeared.'

'You sound overly concerned. Isn't that what you want? Me to disappear?'

Jacques laughs and looks at the floor guiltily.

'Everything all right?' I say. 'Hotel okay?'

'Oh yes,' he looks up at me. 'Everything is fine. I just thought you'd actually done a runner. You know, we had no idea where you were. Even Nancy and the Singaporean guy wouldn't tell us where you were all going. Seemed a bit strange.'

Jacques seems to have an unusual interest in my whereabouts. In fact, it's more than that. He seems to take genuine pleasure in the idea of me running away without a trace.

I leave the hotel and return to my borrowed villa.

Back again. Got the TV. Got the whisky. Got the deli around the corner. Got the girls at Destiny down the road. I feel as depressed as can be. I miss Nancy and Wai Ming. I miss our adventure in the hills. I don't want my old life back. Something has changed.

And by midnight, nothing has changed at all. I'm back at Destiny. I'm passionately drunk. I'm playing pool (very badly) and I'm laughing with the girls. I have an argument with an Australian tourist. He complains about Asia; how they don't respect human rights or the rule of law; how they're all corrupt. He's a pompous sod if ever there was one.

'You better pipe down,' I tell him. 'Can't come swaggering over here, telling them what to do. It's not as if you're American. Like, you know, from a real superpower. All you ever did was invent the windy-dryer. You're just a little country, stuck out there on a desert island. You don't even have enough people to fill up Shanghai. You should pipe down. Really. I mean it.'

He looks at me with a mortified frown. I can tell he's angry. He wants to hit me.

I stagger home, occasionally veering into a drain or a lamppost. I believe all this to be mightily funny. I slump down in an armchair, turn on the TV and pour Scotch down my throat directly from the bottle. I'm sick on the floor.

When I wake up, the house is infested with mosquitoes. I'd left the front door wide open. It's the start of the rainy season and they have emerged from the drains of the city in bloodthirsty clouds. My face lies flat against the cool floor tiles. A cigarette, burnt down to the filter, is still clamped between my stiff yellow fingers. I see the pool of vomit. It's dry around the edges, like a salt pan. I close my eyes. I'll be needing an aspirin.

At around midday I try to Skype Angela. She's a qualified pharmacist, I'll have you know. She works for an American pharmaceutical company, what we like to call Big Pharma. She's a bright thing, Angela. Went to university. Like her mother. It's a weekday. I think it's Tuesday. She'll be working. I look at my watch and try to count five hours back. But I can't work out whether I'm counting backwards or forwards. I'm seized by an infernal confusion! I want to rip the watch from my hand, fling it across the room and smash it against the wall. Fucking thing is tricking me!

So, maybe Angela is not yet at work. Maybe she's *on her way* to work. Or she's dropping Marcus off at school. She's probably very busy. I try to think if it's school holidays. What time of the year is it? When do they take their holidays? I reach no useful conclusion. And why wouldn't her – what do they call him … her *partner?* – why wouldn't he be dropping Marcus off at school? Why is it always the mother who does that? It's the modern world, you know.

I can't reach her. Every time the call fails to connect, Skype gives me that sad note of failure, like some dead thing that has fallen into a pond: *ghaloop!*

I lean back in my chair, staring at the screen. Failed to connect. This statement is far more perturbing than Skype realises. It is more than a mere statement of fact. It awakens in me a profound emotional experience. My river has grown black and tepid, caught in a sluggish swamp. I can't quite make sense of it.

I think of Nancy – slowly dying in a hotel room with a view of a stupa. Follow the symbols, she'd told me.

And when I think of Angela I picture the snake entwined around that stick; the symbol of healing. She used to play in the garden of our block of flats in Durban. She played with the other children and she was always the nurse. She used to make little nurse hats out of paper and draw a red cross on them with a red marker.

She's not in the service of Big Pharma. She is in the service of healing. Why has that been so easily forgotten?

In the late afternoon I walk to the stupa and Wai Ming and Nancy are there.

'Hi!' I say eagerly, striding up towards them as if they are my oldest friends.

They seem pleased to see me too.

We sit near the stupa and Nancy says, 'How are you feeling these days?'

I look down at the fleshy grass beneath me, assailed by the most appalling guilt. 'I don't know,' I say. 'I mean I feel terrible. Trapped. Always trapped.'

'I know,' she says. 'I know that feeling too.'

'And you? How are *you* feeling?'

After a long pause she says, 'Sometimes trapped; trapped in this sick body and sometimes free. I'll know soon enough.'

Wai Ming looks at me and says, 'Where is your river now, Julian?'

I'm glad he asked me about my river because it is precisely what I had envisioned earlier in the day. 'It's in a swamp. It's moving sluggishly through the weeds and the reeds, mixed in with thick black mud, slowly evaporating in the sun, into nothingness.'

'Sounds a bit gloomy.'

'It is gloomy!' I stammer. And then I feel wretched. 'I mean, what am I saying? Here I am talking about gloom, when you're the one who's …' I stop and look up to face Nancy. I can't bring myself to say it.

'Dying?'

'Yes. And I'm all obsessed over my river image.'

'You selfish buffoon,' she says playfully and she laughs.

When they are ready to leave I stand up. I give Wai Ming a brief hug and I give Nancy a gentle squeeze on the shoulder. 'Let me know if there's anything I can do.'

'We will.'

Wai Ming begins to push the wheelchair back to the hotel.

I call after them. 'See you again!'

I do see them again. Every day that week, we meet at the stupa. And with each passing day I see that Nancy is smaller than before; weaker. Her face is more sunken, slowly retreating from the light. Her back is more hunched. Her arms thinner. And she is beginning to slur her speech. The deterioration of her body is marked and rapid.

I still say the most moronic things. 'You're looking better than yesterday.' Or, 'You seem to have a bit more colour!'

They look at me doubtfully.

What had Wai Ming told me when we were at the bar in Vang Vieng? That knowledge is also a kind of ignorance? Here, we all see the same thing: a dying woman in a wheelchair. But it isn't what I see that matters. It's what I *feel about what I see*. This explains the old housewives adage: you can't lie to yourself. Now that really is a shame.

I am sitting at my table in the villa and I'm googling 'craniosacral therapy' when I receive a Skype call. It's Angela!

'Hi Dad, sorry, I got a missed call from you a few days ago. I've been so busy. Run off my feet. Haven't had a chance to call you back. You know how it is. How are you?'

'Fine!' I say with disconcerting sprightliness. 'Absolutely fine.'

'Everything okay?'

'Yip. Fine. Fine.'

'Oh great.'

I can't remember why I had phoned Angela a few days before. What was it that I had wanted to say to her? We sit for a while in silence.

'I mean, how are *you*?' I say. 'I was just checking in to see how you are. How's Marcus and ... and ...' I've forgotten the name of her partner.

'Sean.'

'Oh yes. Sean.'

'We're good. We're all good, you know ...'

'Great. And the job? Keeping busy, I suppose?'

'Oh, it's madness. And Marcus just turned nine. We had a party at the weekend. We had more than twenty people and a jumping castle.'

I laugh. It's a sort of brittle, contrived sound. I've long since stopped being entertained by the thrill of jumping castles. 'I've been thinking about you. Quite a lot.'

'Oh, I've been thinking about you too.'

'You think you might come over to Asia for a visit? I can show you around. They've got temples and ... you know, heaps of things. All the Buddhist stuff. You'd like it.'

'I don't know, Dad. I mean, Sean's parents have moved to Ireland, so we're going there for Christmas. Probably won't be able to do a trip to Asia any time soon.'

Sean's parents live in Ireland. They're going to visit them for

Christmas. She might as well cut my heart out with a cheap steak-knife.

'You married yet?'

'Oh, Dad, I wish you'd stop asking that. We don't … you know, we don't want to do that. People don't do that anymore.'

No, people don't. Even people who *do* get married these days, aren't really getting married. They're just following a convention, fitting in. I'm stricken by a fleeting memory of my wedding day, my marriage to Maureen. We sat at a table in the Roma Revolving Restaurant, thirty-two storeys above the city of Durban. Everyone was chatting and drinking and having a jolly old time. I looked across at Maureen. She held her knife and fork. I remember being surprised to see that ring on her finger. I'd put it there that very morning. The rings. That's where all the meaning is. I ended up selling mine at a pawn shop. Needed the money.

Angela and I talk about the drought in Cape Town. We talk about the corruption of the state. We talk about whether there might be a better place for them to live. They were thinking about Ireland.

As the call reaches its natural end I say, 'Hey, Angela, remember when you were little? We were living at the flat on the Berea. You used to play in the garden with your friends. Remember how you always played the nurse? You used to make those little nurse hats out of paper. Remember?'

There is a long silence.

Finally she says, 'Not at all. I don't remember that. Me? A nurse?'

'That was your thing.'

'Oh I doubt it.' She laughs.

I tell her that I love her.

There is another long silence.

'Dad, are you sure you're okay?'

'Fine! Fine! Absolutely fine.'

I'm half gladdened and half annoyed by this call.

That evening, back at the stupa, I tell Nancy and Wai Ming that I'd spoken to Angela.

'Oh good,' Nancy says. She drawls.

'Yes. She's fine.'

They can hear the note of doubt in my voice.

'Fine?' says Wai Ming.

'Well, I don't know.' I let out a heavy sigh. 'I'm glad I spoke to her. But it seems ... it seems ... that the best part of the call was the silence; when we were just on each end of the line, sitting in silence.'

'Ah!' he replies. 'The music is not in the notes, but in the silence between.'

'Another one of your ancient Chinese sayings, is it?'

'Not at all. It might have been Beethoven. Or maybe it even comes from an American cigarette ad. I forget, but definitely not Chinese. We could google it if we wanted to avoid an argument.'

'Oh, it's not worth arguing over.'

'True. So little is. You almost wonder if the Information Age is really worth it,' he offers his high-pitched, warbling laugh.

When they are about to leave, Wai Ming has taken hold of the handles of the wheelchair, Nancy raises her hand slowly. I see, as her shawl falls away from it, how thin it is, how the mottled skin hangs loosely from the bones.

'I suppose I was a bit hard on you when we first met,' she says.

'You were?'

'I called you a fool or something like that.'

'Oh, I've been called worse. And frankly, I must have deserved it. For God's sake, look at how I treated you! Abominably!'

'Well, now that all I get to do is look back, it doesn't seem to matter how you treated me. You'll never get anyone to like you, or to love you. That's up to them. It's never really about how they treated you. All you have in the end is how you treated them.'

13

Our ritual at the stupa every evening is somewhat altered the next time around.

As I approach them from the other side of the road, Wai Ming stands up abruptly and walks towards me. The man, although I could not see his face in the shadows, is plainly exhausted.

'She's in terrible pain,' he explains softly. 'I don't know what more we can do. The morphine is not enough.'

He stands in front of me – a forlorn creature if ever there was one. He leans slightly towards me as if he might soon clutch on to me. I take a step back, not sure I want that.

I look beyond him and see Nancy in her chair. She is more hunched than ever and I wonder if that is a slightly deranged sort of whimper I hear? Does she quiver slightly beneath her shawl?

'I … I think I've got an idea!' I say brightly. It's my old exit plan. 'We can get something stronger. Stronger than morphine. I can get some. It's no problem.'

'What? What do you mean?'

I lean towards him confidingly. 'Leave it to me. It's the business. She won't know herself!'

It is time for me to put my long-standing plan into action, not for me, but someone I know: the most powerful painkiller known to humankind – even an illegal one. Despite my bullish assurances to Wai Ming, I have no idea how to go about it.

I head to Destiny.

'I've these two friends,' I say to John.

'Really?' He is incredulous.

'Yes, well it's not that surprising.'

'Well, it surprises me,' he sneers.

'Well, the thing is that one of them is dying of cancer. She's at an advanced stage. She's in massive pain.'

'Oh,' he says. I can tell he wants to say more. Something like, Oh God, or Oh fuck, or Oh no. But he doesn't. That's John Webb. Likes to appear as if he's as tough as nuts.

'The thing is I've always had a plan that if that ever happened to me, cancer I mean, I would immediately rush out and buy … you know … a painkiller – something super strong.'

'That's a plan.'

'Even something illegal.'

'Like what?'

I shrug.

There is a long pause and John looks up from his drink with a sly smile. 'Are you asking me if I know how to score heroin in this town?'

'Well … I … I mean, do you?'

'I'm not sure. I don't think it's easy. They're strict about that stuff over here. Sex tourists and drugs addicts aren't really their thing.' He turns away and stares sadly at his drink. 'But I guess it's for a good cause. A woman in terrible pain.'

'It is.'

'Let me see. I know some people. Every country has its dodgy operators.'

About half an hour later John returns. He sits on his regular barstool and, as dispirited as ever, he orders another Pastis.

'Well?'

'Heroin is heavy business. Death penalty stuff. It's not easy. Sorry. I can't help you.'

I lean, exhausted, against the bar counter, morose and helpless. I think of ordering a drink, many drinks in quick succession. But I don't. I stand up wearily. 'Thanks for trying, John.'

'It's no bother. I'm sorry about your friend.'

I walk slowly back to the hotel thinking of Nancy, her abominable pain, her pointed frailty, her decay.

In the driveway of the hotel, I stop and look up at the vaunted building. There is a faded patch of greyish light emanating from the window of Suite 604. The moon is up and I catch fragments of her shape from behind the needle-like black fronds of a palm tree.

Death penalty stuff. Of course it is. How game I am to place my sorry life at risk for Nancy, the old shrew! How quick, how bracing is my remorse, my concern for this woman!

Entering the lobby I stride towards the elevators and I see Farr, the night manager, advance towards me from my office beneath the staircase.

'Good evening, sir,' he says.

'Good evening, Farr. How are you, my good man?'

He glances down at his glossy shoes, seems painfully embarrassed

'Everything all right?'

He looks up. His face reddens. He smiles limply and says,

'Can I help you?'

'*Help* me?'

I detect a slight quaver in his voice. He can't look me in the eye. 'Yes, I mean, the elevators are for the guests. I ... I was told that you're not supposed to go there. Sorry, sir.'

'I'm not supposed to go there? What the hell are you talking about? I'm the fucking general manager of this hotel and I can go wherever the hell I please.'

Farr looks again at his shoes.

'Who told you this?' I continue. 'Mr Jacques? Mr Jacques told you this?'

He nods, still looking at the floor with mortal shame.

'Well, you tell that little prick that I will be here in the morning and I will fire his arse. Right? You tell him I'll be here first thing and I'll have him packing.'

I storm on towards the elevators, muttering to myself: *I'm the fucking general manager! The sheer insolence of it!*

In Suite 604 they have moved a single bed into the living room, which is where Wai Ming sleeps. In the bedroom, Nancy is just a shrivelled, broken bird-like figure under the sheets.

'Shhh,' Wai Ming says. 'She is sleeping. She gets so little sleep because of the pain.'

He quietly closes the door to her room and we sit on his bed.

'I'm sorry. I can't get anything for the pain. I thought it would be easy, but it's not. I thought I might be able to get some heroin.'

'Heroin?' Wai Ming is startled. 'That's illegal!'

My dear Singaporean friend, he makes me laugh sombrely. They're a rather orderly lot, those Singaporeans.

'You know what they call three people jay-walking in Singapore?'

'What?'

'A crime wave.'

He laughs. I laugh. We are both very close to crying.

'It's all right, Julian,' he says at last. 'In life you only have one real practical responsibility.'

'And that is?'

'Do the best you can with what you have.'

Before I leave, I open the door and peep into Nancy's bedroom. She is in the same position as before, still sleeping in that sullen light. Such a shrunken figure, even the thin sheet seems to lie heavily upon her. She's in that dream world. Her body breathes dutifully, audibly while she is in that incomprehensible place – that place of not knowing; of little more than mysterious images. She follows the symbols.

Returning to the living room, now Wai Ming's living quarters, I say, 'See you.'

He nods. As I walk down the corridor, these words, *see you*, echo in my head and carry with them a strange and novel resonance. How easily we utter these things.

The following morning I advance to the Samarang Hotel with great purpose. I've dressed in one of my collared shirts and a pair of shiny slacks and I'm wearing my polished black work shoes. I've even applied a dash of cologne. Yes, my hair is distinctively grey (I've stopped using the colouring), but I need to look my best in order to confront my hapless underling: little Jacques.

Sith doffs his cap. I snap my heels together and give him a

military salute. He laughs out loud. I stride to my office under the staircase. I push open the door and there he is! At my desk! My ashtray holds a little pile of paperclips!

'What the fuck do you think you're doing?'

He blinks at me. Seems a little astonished.

'Farr tells me that I'm not allowed in the elevators. Apparently you told him.'

'You're on suspension,' he stammers.

'Suspension, yes. But I am still the fucking general manager of this hotel and I go where I very well please.'

Jacques stands uneasily.

'And what the fuck are you doing sitting at my desk? That's *my* fucking desk.'

He raises his hands in a sort of futile gesture of surrender. 'Please,' he says, 'calm down.'

'No I will not calm down. That's the last thing you should expect of me. I have a friend dying upstairs and I will visit her whenever I please. And the last fucking thing I need is your bloody permission!'

With an unexpected steely resolve and a deliberate smirk he says, 'I happen to be the *acting* general manager for the moment.'

'While not when I'm in the building. When I'm here, you're just acting; acting up or acting out. Just a little fraud. You're nothing. I'll have you fired in a … a …' I snap my fingers in the air.

'Well, I'm sorry to tell you that this comes from Mr Lim. Remember him? The owner? If you want to quarrel about this, you can do it with Mr Lim directly.'

Quarrel? Strange word. These foreigners!

'Mr Lim? Fine. I'll take it up with him. In the meantime, I suggest you pack your bags.'

He still has that smirk on his face; the face I feel like punching or smacking with the flat end of a spade.

'What the fuck is it about the French!' I say at last, turn on my heel and storm out of the building.

That afternoon I'm back at the villa. I'm watching TV and I've had a few beers. I'm sitting in my underpants on the sofa. My paunch sags miserably over my tufted crotch. I'm sweating under the ceiling fan. I have no idea what I'm watching.

I see out the window that Mr Lim's black Lexus has silently arrived. I jump into action, racing around to find clothing. By the time he is knocking at the front door, I am struggling with my trousers which twist and snag around my lumpy legs, as if they're refusing to have anything to do with me. 'In a minute!' I say.

I smoothen my hair in the mirror. Fully clothed, with no shoes I answer the door.

'Ah, Mr Juwy!' His narrow eyes sparkle and his smile is just as forgiving and amiable as it always was.

'Hello, Mr Lim.'

He peers into the gloomy interior as if peeping into the cave of a potentially dangerous bear. 'I come in?'

'Yes, yes, of course.' I hurry to turn the TV off. 'Can I get you a beer?'

He laughs gently. 'No thank, Mr Juwy. You always the good host. Always offer the drink.'

'Yes,' I laugh sheepishly. I could do with a drink right now. A good old stiff Scotch.

Mr Lim sits in an armchair in the living room. He crosses his legs leisurely. 'So, Mr Juwy. You okay?'

'Okay? Yes, yes, fine. Absolutely fine. I mean it's good to have this time off. You know I've been very busy at the hotel. A lot of stress. I've never taken sick leave. Never taken a holiday. Not once in six years!' I laugh, as if surprised by my own impeccable record of service.

'Ahhh, yes, good to have the holiday.'

'Yes.'

'How about you drinking? You still like drinking so much, yes?'

We both look at the beer cans on the coffee table. In a pique of mindless folly I'd stacked them one upon the other in teetering towers in the same way that I used to do with wooden blocks when I was a kid.

'Yes, I mean, I do. But not much, you know. These cans? Oh, I like to keep them. Play this ... you know ... little ... silly game.' I gulp.

Mr Lim has no idea what I'm talking about. He wants to change the subject. He leans back in his chair and looks out the window, waiting for me to stop.

Finally, after a weighty pause, he says, 'So you want to come back working?'

'Yes!' I say exultantly, but I know that's not really true. I'm acting. I'm surprisingly credible.

'Ah, good, good,' he smiles and faces me directly. 'You sure you no want to go home?'

'Home? Oh, Mr Lim, the Samarang is my home. It's been my

home for six years!'

'Ah, yes. I know. You good manager, Mr Juwy. Is okay. You rest more. Take easy time, okay?' He stands. He's an old man with a stoop. Standing isn't what it was. It's become a sort of uneasy totter.

He walks to the door. 'Oh, and Mr Juwy, your friend, Miss Neecie.'

'Nancy.'

'Yes, Ms Neecie. She okay. You visit her, is okay. Anytime. She very sick. She asking for dying at the Samarang. I say okay. She your friend. You take care her, okay?' he suddenly breaks into his familiar broad smile and gives me his familiar encouraging pat on the back. 'You the good manager, Mr Juwy.'

'Yes,' I say, closing the door behind him. I return to my living room muttering under my breath: that'll be *general* manager, actually.

They no longer visit the stupa.

So, now that I have it on the highest possible authority – Mr Lim himself – I am free to wander about the Samarang at will. Jacques be damned!

Entering the room, Wai Ming speaks in a whisper. 'She's awake. You've arrived at a good time.'

A good time. These words hang awkwardly between us. What vast parameters they cover!

'I'm glad to hear it,' I say.

I walk with deliberate caution into her darkened room.

'Julian,' she says. 'So good to see you.' Her words are slurred and there is a daunting kind of hollowness to them.

'Good to see you too, Nancy.'

I sit on the side of her bed. She is just a girl. A small withered girl.

'Not long to go now.'

I can't say anything. I feel that lump in my throat. I offer just a slight squeaking noise.

She lifts her skeletal arm above the sheet and searches for my hand. She holds it and we sit in silence for some time. I can't tell if she has drifted off to sleep. Her mouth hangs open. It's just a dark oval crater; an empty space on her gaunt face.

'Wai Ming told me what you tried to do.'

'What?'

'The heroin.'

Just a subtle twitch of her lips was all that remained of her smile. How she was even capable of such a thing, a smile, confounded me.

'Oh, it's … nothing. I mean I'm sorry I couldn't get any.'

'It's all right. I will be taken to the end on the wings of pain. Death becomes the last remaining source of relief.'

I give her hand a gentle squeeze.

'You're a very courageous person.'

'We are all courageous in the end, Julian.' A little dribble runs from the corner of her mouth. I snatch a tissue out of the box on the side table and wipe it away.

'Where is Wai Ming?' she says as I crumple up the damp tissue and put it in my pocket.

'I'm here.' Wai Ming stands at the door behind me.

'Oh, will you open the safe? Remember what we talked

about?'

'Yes.' Wai Ming walks to the wardrobes and I hear the little electronic beeps as he presses the buttons of the safe.

Nancy says, 'I have some money left and I want you to have it.'

She wants to say more, but seems too exhausted.

'I ... that's ... I mean, it's okay. You don't need to.'

'I want to.'

Wai Ming returns from the safe. With a distinctively ceremonial air he hands me a neat stack of Euros.

'It's all that's left,' Nancy says. Her head twitches slightly to the left, trying to make out Wai Ming in the gloom. 'How much is there, Wai Ming?'

'It's thirty thousand.'

'Thirty thousand,' she repeats. She returns to face me. She smiles. I can see that she'd like to laugh. 'I'm sorry it's not more.'

I can't say anything. I lean towards her, still holding her fragile hand and rest my head gently on her chest. I hear her heart. I hear her breathe. The phantom-like rhythm of life still stirs inside her; the whole pulsating episode of her story is slowly weakening, shifting, strumming ever further away towards its own needful end.

Before I leave, as I am about to stand, Nancy's feeble hold on my wrist tightens a little, not much more than a weak pulse. Still, I can sense that typical firmness, the unyielding strength of her body. She says something, but I cannot make it out. I lean closer. I can feel her breath against my ear. 'Death,' she says, 'is a difficult thing. One of many. And this one is the last one.'

14

I visit Nancy every day.

Jacques is sometimes in the lobby and he scowls at me. I give him my most winning smile.

Wai Ming says, 'It's hard to tell. It could be today. Or next week. The week after next. The final clue is always in the breathing. I follow the breathing.'

This remark – I follow the breathing – excites in me a rather unusual contemplation of what it is to breathe. We inhale this essential gas and we exhale nothing but poison. Why do we do that? Exhale poison? What does it mean? What does it ... *symbolize*?

That afternoon I am watching cable TV. A European country has got its knickers in a knot over the burkha. Why do they do that? What's that all about? The burkha ban? I don't get it. I've never got it.

I put this to John Webb later that night.

'It's something to do with the oppression of women,' he says.

'But banning it!' I say. 'I mean it's just an item of clothing, like a hat. It's not, you know, some kind of weapon of mass destruction.'

'I know. The stupid thing is that *all* clothing is oppression. Whether it's a bikini or a burkha. It makes no difference. It's all oppressive; an oppressive system designed to crimp our most primitive urges; conceal our reddish bits so we don't rush around like maniacs, poking this and that with wild abandon. We don't trust ourselves, our instincts, so we oppress them instead. The burkha ban? It's just our usual arrogance. As if we've worked out the good oppression from the bad.'

'So what are you saying? We should all be swaggering around in the nude?' I laugh loudly at the idea of it. It even arouses me slightly – primitive beast that I am.

But John is not amused. He's never amused. He's a writer, remember?

'Not really,' he says. 'The idea of concealment is a good one. It offers us a suggestion of what we *might* be like beneath our skimpy or elaborate drapery. We do not get to construe the body in a literal way. We get to *imagine* it. It's what makes metaphor so powerful. It's the mystery of it that inspires our imagination; makes the human experience so rewarding. It's the mystery. The *not* knowing.'

After a short pause, I say. 'Not the facts.'

John looks up from his drink and studies me closely. He offers me a slightly grim smile. 'Yes,' he says. 'Have you ever taken a really close look at pussy? The cock and balls? The anus? The blotchy nipples? The foul-smelling effluvia? Studied all that in detail, have you? No, definitely not the facts.'

I am comfortably out of my mind as I saunter back to the villa that night. I think about oblivion – not knowing – the drugs and the booze. We love it all right. All over the world. Even those Muslims with their burkhas, they love a bit of booze. They say they're not supposed to have it, but that's not the same as saying they don't *like* it. So is that it? Is that what we do? Stumble through life in drunken oblivion? Somehow it seems a bit too smart. A bit too handy. Somehow undeserved, like a trick of which we are the perpetrator and the victim.

And then I think of Nancy. Nancy and her wings of pain.

True. I wake up with a headache.

Pot smokers tell me – a bit smugly – that pot doesn't give you a headache. For that reason, it is infinitely superior to booze. And I've smoked enough of it to know that's true. But do you know what I don't like about pot? It stops you from dreaming. When you smoke pot, day after day, you won't dream when you sleep. There is, somewhere in all of that, an element of evasion.

I know exactly when Nancy dies. I know this because I look at my watch. It's 12.01.

But I am not there with her. I am not in her room.

I am standing – rather unexpectedly – in front of the stupa. I'd taken a detour as I returned from the deli on my way home and now I am standing in front of the stupa, gazing up at its slightly crooked spire, pointing awkwardly at an unknowable universe – beyond the universe perhaps. It's a very old, crumbling edifice – now forms the rather grandiose centrepiece of a quiet, downtown traffic circle.

It is a hot, still day. The sluggish air of this slow-moving town, does not dare stir. The shadows of the stupa have shrunk inward, almost disappeared. I want to walk on, but I don't. I feel the weight of my shopping bags pulling me towards the ground. I hear the clink of the gin and the whisky bottles as I place them on the grass, releasing them from my anxious grip. Still standing, I am struck by a sudden breeze. And now I know that Nancy is dead. It has a strange forcefulness, this breeze – warm at first and then it grows cooler. I accept it with relief. I feel it press against my skin as it sweeps through the shimmering square, caresses the corroded old stupa and presents its ghost-like whispers in the narrow spaces of the old house in which Nancy was born.

I know it's her.

I kneel down. I press my face to the grass. Feel the warmth of the earth on my forehead. A sob rises to my throat.

'Thank you,' I say. 'Thank you for your story.'

I do not say her name.

15

What John Webb had told me about the power of metaphor has stuck with me. It would not have done so had Nancy not once appealed to me to follow the symbols.

I find myself pondering this – almost each moment of the day: the symbol of the wind and the rain; the symbol of day and night, of breathing and the beating of the heart, of the magnetism of the moon; of light and shadow. Try as we might, we have no consciousness without symbolism – this awareness that the things we see, the experiences we encounter, always represent something other than themselves.

When Nancy died, something happened to my river image. As I have said before, over the preceding weeks the flow of the water had slowed, sunk into the mud and had formed a stagnant, tepid swamp; its fluidity imperceptible. It gave off a fetid smell. And the moment Nancy died, at a discreet point where the water lapped weakly at the muddy fringes, a small clod of earth collapsed, opening up a slight chasm. Water began to trickle forward, through the little gap, in a single silvery thread, winding its way through the yellow stalks of the reeds and slowly gathering momentum as it descended into a shaded valley.

Whenever I talk to people about my river image, they think I'm nuts. The problem, you see, is that they are stricken by a nut image.

I have stashed my crisp stack of Euros on a ceiling board above the dining room table.

I don't have much money. Have never earned much, never saved much. Whenever I think about my retirement I feel like a drink. More than one. I do not have access to a welfare state, a pension fund, or money that *makes money*. I'll have to work forever. Do you know that the next best alternative – I've given this a lot of thought – is for me to fly to Sweden and commit a heinous crime? I'll go out and murder a few kids. It's a suitably appalling crime. I'm sure I'll find some miscreants who make a nuisance of themselves and who deserve an early departure. But still, they'll be kids, young people, and I'll go off and murder them. And then I'll be arrested and put in one of those luxury Swedish prisons for the rest of my life. They've got pool tables and ping-pong tables. They've got flat-screen TVs and free beer at lunchtime. There are fully equipped gymnasiums with spa baths and saunas, and you get a weekly visit from a pretty female therapist with long, unblemished legs who listens attentively to your story and makes notes about you on a clipboard. They even offer classes where you can learn how to write computer code or how to play the violin. I know all this because I saw it in a documentary. It's better than an underfunded, state-sponsored home for the indigent in downtown Durban – that's for sure. It's better than begging on the streets of Harare.

So far, that is the most promising retirement plan I have. And so this money comes in handy. I promise myself that I shall not waste it. I've done that before. God knows. But now I know that

I won't be getting any second chances. Thirty thousand Euros is a lot of money.

Unbeknown to me, Wai Ming had been diligent in organizing a ceremony for Nancy. I had given the logistics some thought myself. As the general manager I had contemplated the call that would need to be made to the consular people at the British Embassy. They would need to arrange the removal of the body – just as the Russians had done for poor Mr Andropov. Mr Lim might insist on yet another Buddhist ceremony in Suite 604. And that would be that. Life at the Samarang would carry on swimmingly.

But Wai Ming had done more. He'd visited the local temple. He'd discussed the matter with a senior monk and Nancy's body would be cremated with the usual trappings afforded the dead in this part of the world. I can't say that Nancy was a Buddhist. I'd never heard her describe herself in that way, but I did think it rather decent of the Buddhist monk to afford her a Buddhist ceremony. Then again, perhaps that is what Buddhists do. Perhaps they're not quite so hysterical about those who are and those who are not 'members of the faith'. Wai Ming had arranged the artefacts – the last remaining possessions – that would accompany Nancy's body in the casket. And he had arranged the casket itself. He'd also contacted the British Embassy to assist with the removal of the body. It was now in a local hospital.

The ceremony is scheduled for the day after tomorrow.

'It can't be tomorrow,' Wai Ming explains. 'Tomorrow is a full moon.'

'Right.' I have no idea why this might be relevant.

He is packing his things into a small bag.

'I'll need to check out of here,' Wai Ming says as he folds one of his shirts, smoothens it out carefully with a delicate brownish hand.

'But the suite is booked and paid for, at least until the end of the month as far as I recall. She went sooner than she thought.'

'I know, but she has only a little money left in her account and I promised her I would save it. Donate the final balance to the temple.'

'Oh, well ...' I pause and consider the ramifications. 'There'll be a late cancellation fee, you know.'

'I suppose so.'

Throughout the ordeal of Nancy's demise, Wai Ming had remained such an orderly soul. He had attended to Nancy with such dedication, such professionalism that I'd scarcely considered whether any of this might have distressed him.

He zips up his little bag, sighs deeply and then turns and sits heavily on the bed. He leans forward, puts his hands up to his face and sits very still. I see the tips of his ears redden.

I gulp. I shift my weight from one foot to the other. I have nothing to say.

Finally he looks up at me with slightly moist eyes. 'You know, in this country they call a house where a person dies a "good house". And the house where a person is born is called a "bad house". Did you know that?'

'No. I didn't. Seems like they've got it the wrong way around, haven't they?'

He smiles at me weakly. 'That's what I thought when I first

learned of it. But no, this is quite deliberate. The point of it of course, is that birth marks the beginning of suffering and death marks the end. The symbolism of these two houses – the bad house and the good house – prompts action, it prompts inaction. It guides you towards compassion and protects you from self-obsession.'

He stands and lifts his bag from the bed, placing the strap over his shoulder.

'I'll be flying back to Singapore after the cremation. I'm so grateful for everything you've done, Julian. Nancy was a special friend. I know she was grateful too. You were exactly what she needed.'

He puts his hand out and I shake it, but I feel that his gratitude is entirely undeserved. I'd been nothing but a whiny, self-obsessed, bombastic buffoon. Hadn't I?

'Oh, I've done nothing. I mean, I feel a bit awful quite frankly. I could have done so much more. Been a bit less, you know, selfish. Funny, on the day that we got back from Phou Nang Fa, Nancy said to me: I'm glad you were the one. I had no idea what she meant. And now here you are telling me that I am exactly what she needed. I … I don't really get it.'

We are walking down the corridor, towards the elevators.

'It's kind of a hard thing to do at first, but what Nancy meant – and I say this as a student of hers and not a very good one – is that everyone we meet, no matter the circumstances, is always the right person for that moment. We all carry a symbolic meaning for the other. It is only up to us to examine ourselves and find out what that meaning is.'

I press the down arrow for the elevator. 'Oh, I've heard all that before. Examine the self. Self discovery, self awareness, *finding* the self. It's all a bit vague to me. No one seems to know what it means. How the hell do you examine yourself? Staring in a mirror will only get you so far.'

Wai Ming gives me that odd girlish laugh again. 'No. You won't see very much of yourself in a mirror. That's true. But you will always see yourself in others. We're not as solitary as we like to think. I think Nancy might already have told you: Your story. My story. Their story. The first thing you will realise is that it's all one story. It's our story. Isn't that what she said?'

'Yes. So she did.'

'We are all symbols to each other. And the whole point of symbols is that we can only *imagine* their meaning. A symbol has no meaning in itself. Your life therefore has no meaning to *you*. If you want to appreciate what your life means – if it means anything at all – you will only do so by appreciating what it means to others.' As the old elevator shudders towards the ground floor, returning us to the earth, Wai Ming adds, 'Your river image. Don't forget your river image. Life is a mysterious thing. It'd be a pity if all we ever did was try to explain it.'

We part in the lobby. I stand there, surrounded by large oil paintings on the walls and neatly clipped fan palms in polished ceramic pots. Clumps of guests mutter to each other, waiting for their taxis. I watch Wai Ming leave through the swing doors and walk down the driveway for a cheaper place to stay. He's a solitary figure, if not lonely.

Now, on the day of the funeral, I see that there are more

symbols than you can poke a stick at down at the Buddhist temple. I see gargoyles and horned dragons, effigies of the Buddha, of Chinese deities, of Hindu deities. I see garudas, hanumans, winged apsaras, and murals on the ceiling in vivid colours detailing aspects of the Buddha's journey, festooned with lotus flowers and banyan trees beyond which appear mythical bearded creatures and elfin-like forest dwellers. I wonder what all this means. The forces of good and evil. The impermanence of matter. The unity of opposites. I'm not sure, but I feel drawn to the images in a way that I've not felt before.

I suppose there are many traditions that present similar or similarly complex imagery. I've never been a fan. Always thought it to be a bit opaque; as if deliberately so, because behind all the obfuscation they know there is nothing. Isn't that what they always tell us? God works in mysterious ways? I've always regarded that as the most monstrous cop out. But now I'm not sure. What might I have been expecting? That God ought to work in a literal way? Like some sort of lecturer? Or some sort of health and safety manager? A tech guru? Where would that leave me? Where would that leave my life? What is this conscious experience of living if we are not searching for meaning?

And there is Nancy's casket. Rising from each corner are thin, white-painted poles that hold a sort of canopy aloft. White translucent fabric hangs from the canopy, flowing slightly in the gentle breeze. The casket rests on a concrete plinth with a hollow passage beneath it that is filled with firewood. I grimace at the idea of it being set alight.

The cicadas, from their shaded spots, are at their most

piercing. It's a sound that seems to exacerbate the heat. I feel my brow sweating.

We, the congregation, or the mourners – if that is what we are, it doesn't seem like it – are sitting on the tiled floor of a building in the temple grounds. The building is open on three sides and we face the closed side which is adorned with an assemblage of Buddha images along the wall.

Mr Lim and Wai Ming sit on each side of me. Alongside Mr Lim sits an elderly man whom I do not recognise.

I turn to see who else is of our party. I see Sith, the doorman with whom Nancy had once parleyed over the door-opening procedures at the hotel, and Khek the receptionist who'd checked Nancy in all those months ago. I recognize some of the cleaning and housekeeping staff – no doubt they had attended to Nancy through her dying days. Even Jacques, the so-called acting general manager is here. I am pricked by an unusually sentimental gratitude for their attendance at Nancy's funeral. I consider for a moment that collegial team spirit of the Samarang Gang and how – in the final analysis, when all is said and done – they're a fine bunch of people. Except Jacques. Obviously.

Beyond these familiar faces, I see another face, also familiar but not pleasingly so. It's Charles Brinton, the man from the British Embassy. He winks at me and smiles in his usual matey way. I return to face the front. What's he doing here? Yes, Nancy was a British subject so perhaps it's not entirely out of order for an embassy staff member to attend her funeral. But wasn't he something to do with economic affairs? Isn't he, to put all clumsy decoys aside, a British intelligence officer? This is who they send to the funeral? The embassy's resident spy?

A long line of monks in their usual striking orange robes, file into the building. They take their places on a raised platform before us. The elderly man who sits next to Mr Lim addresses the monks. I have no idea what is being said, but I discern the word 'Neecie'. This is uttered a number of times and I know he speaking of Nancy.

The monks begin to pray and as I bow forward with my palms pressed together I feel oddly comforted by the chant; this dependable rhythm; this answer to the turmoil of consciousness. My river glides in green glinting hues through a sunlit valley, in wide expansive curves while light slithers and vibrates on her surface. I don't want the chanting to end. I get the feeling that I might simply want to kneel here, let them chant until I eventually topple over for good. I am heartened each time the chanting seems to dip and slow, and then promptly resumes with renewed vigour onward forever.

I'm in a bit of a daze, when I am called upon by Wai Ming to stand up and walk from the building to the casket. I am accompanied by Mr Lim and Sith and Khek. Each of us takes up a position at a corner of the pyre. Khek accompanies me, while Mr Lim, Wai Ming and Sith take the other three corners on their own.

'I here to help you. In case of you don't know how to do,' says Khek.

I am suddenly alarmed by the possibility that it is my duty to set the pyre alight. I couldn't do it! I cringe and think that I might suddenly want to withdraw, run off into the forested edges of the temple grounds, hide behind the wall of sound offered by the cicadas.

But no, I do not set it alight. Instead I am handed a set of brand new folded robes, of the type worn by the monks. I obey Khek's instructions and kneel down before the casket and I place the robes on the edge of the plinth. Four of the monks appear to have followed us and each of them takes up one of the corners. They resume with their chanting. Khek hands me a bottle of water. When the chanting stops, I unscrew the cap and begin to pour water slowly onto the ground, watch it as it soaks into the earth.

Now the ceremony comes to an end. The others follow and take small bowls of scented water and pour it onto the casket.

As I watch this I fumble in my pocket. It's still there. The tissue I'd used to wipe the spittle from her chin. I draw it out of my pocket and examine it closely. I know now that I had loved Nancy. She'd told me that I'd know love; that I'd wanted to know it.

I walk towards the casket and placed the tissue amidst the yellow blossoms.

We are all courageous in the end.

We – all of us, the people of the Samarang, the occupants of a 'good house' – we all stand back and then two young men arrive with a small tank of gasoline.

Here it goes.

I know I've never seen anything quite like this. I picture Nancy's body. I feel a sob rise to my throat. I am reminded to breathe. The whir of the cicadas holds me steady.

As the pyre begins to spark and crackle, with the smell of combustible fuel thick in the air, smoke curling from the crevices and flames flickering up the edges of the fabric that hang along the sides of the casket, something very strange and unexpected happens to my river. I feel it as sure as it touches my own body. I feel a coolness all along my left side. And I physically turn my head to see what it is. It is another river. It has descended from the mountains, from far in the fading distance. It joins me. Its waters are clearer than my own. There are swirls and eddies and a frisson of disarray as the two bodies of water shudder at this unexpected encounter and slowly they merge into one and it continues on its way.

I feel very good about this. I feel very grateful for the woman we all called Nancy.

I hear her words, 'I'm glad it was you.'

Our stories are one.

16

Wai Ming has his small bag hanging from his shoulder and he is heading towards the temple gates. He is telling me about the time he served at this temple as a novice monk. He'd come here in his thirties, learned the language and obtained admission to the temple for a period of three months.

I'm having difficulty listening to him.

The silence of the place – after the momentous spitting, fizzing and crackling of the giant burning pyre – is now emphatic, almost numbing. Even the cicadas have fallen silent. It is Nancy's silence that hangs over me and Wai Ming's voice comes to me as if from a great distance.

There is also the presence of Charles Brinton. I can sense him following us close behind and I dare not look around. I can feel he has an urgent need to speak to me while I have an urgent need to avoid him.

'When I was a novice,' Wai Ming says, 'the senior monk, the same one who presided today, told me that I need not observe any of the rules. I was a bit astounded. We were supposed to wake early, attend morning prayers, meditate, collect alms, eat breakfast together, clean the temple grounds, eat lunch together, meditate and attend evening prayers. But he simply said that if I did none of those things, it was of no concern to him. I couldn't quite understand how this was supposed to work if no one obeyed the rules. He simply said, "You'll need to decide what kind of monk you want to be". I've never forgotten that. The same question confronts us all.'

'Right,' I say. But I haven't really been listening. Charles Brinton has moved ever closer and he is walking slowly, just as we are.

Wai Ming stops at the gates and turns to face me. He puts out his hand, 'Well, Julian, this is where we say farewell. I am so grateful to have met you.'

I shake his hand, slightly mortified by the swiftness of his departure, even though I ought to have expected it. He'd told me he would be leaving directly after the cremation. But it all seems to be happening too fast.

'You off to the airport?'

'Yes. Time for home.'

'I'll go with you! I mean to the airport. I can hail a cab!'

Wai Ming gives me his usual laugh. 'It's all right. It's time for me to wander on, along my lonely path.'

I turn and face him squarely. I glare at him, almost envious of him. With nothing further to say, I step forward abruptly and put my arms around him, hold him close to me. I don't want him to go. He is going to leave me here. Nancy is dead – her body just a heap of powder, slowly growing cold beneath the smouldering embers on the plinth. It's just me, and *my* lonely path; the path I can't abide.

Wai Ming pats me gently on the back. 'Thank you,' he says. 'Thank you for everything.'

He walks through the dim archway of the temple gate into the street and hails a cab.

I stand under the archway, more alone than ever. I feel as if I've just lost a friend. I haven't felt like this since I was nine, or ten, or something like that.

'Friend of yours?'

I turn and Charles Brinton is much closer to me than I'd thought. He has a slightly off-putting grin on his pinched face.

'You work it out.'

I turn and walk through the temple gates. I walk at a slightly hastened pace.

'I just popped in to pay my respects to Nancy. A British subject, of course. You know how we are.'

'I'm not sure I do.'

Charles laughs. 'The embassy was involved of course. You know, we had to remove the body and so on. It's only fair that we send a representative to honour her memory. A very lovely lady by all accounts.'

'You mean the economic affairs advisor? Or the embassy spook? That's who you send to honour the dead? Why is that? Make sure that they are, in fact, dead? Cross them off the list, send a report to say that they're no longer a security threat to the realm?'

'Ha, not quite.' He is struggling to keep up with me and I'm slightly pleased by that. 'I suppose you've seen right through me. No, I'm not here for the dead, that's true. I'm here for the living.'

I stop.

He catches up to me. He seems remarkably unfit for a spy; for someone with a license to kill.

He peers at me closely. He still has that slightly sneering expression. 'You've been away. Couldn't quite work out where you might have gone. It was a bit troubling. Thought you might have done a runner. The kind of thing expected of a guilty man.'

'Of course, I'm guilty. We're all fucking guilty. Yes, I did do a runner. I took Nancy to Phou Nang Fa.'

'Yes, I know that now, but we didn't know it then, did we?'

'You're a condescending little prick.'

'And being suspended from your job? What's with that? Seemed odd. It was just a day after you and I spoke. I thought I'd told you quite plainly not to make any sudden moves. And so you promptly leave your job and hide out in a little villa. And then you disappear for five days.'

'It's none of your fucking business.'

'You seem to be forgetting that we're on the same side, Julian. I'm looking out for you. Those Russians have an eye on you, still.'

'Still?'

Charles looks around apprehensively. 'We can't talk here. I'll pop in again sometime. We'll have a Scotch together. But for God's sake man, we're on the same side!'

Charles Brinton suddenly turns on his heel and marches back to the temple. The sun is already down, the shadows long on the ground and the bats are already coursing with their usual skittishness across a smoky evening sky.

I return to my villa. It must be said that I like this villa. It was built in the 60s, or maybe even the 50s, in the final days of French occupation. It has wooden shutters and no glass in the windows

– only mosquito gauze. There is a small staircase at the end of the front room that leads to one large bedroom with polished wooden floors upstairs. The walls are all white with distinct patches of bubbling yellow damp in the corners. Translucent geckos lie flat against them, in an almost catatonic stupor. Downstairs there is a small room next to the kitchen. It has a desk and a chair and I have claimed it as my study. The air conditioner is an enormous contraption embedded in the wall. Made in the Soviet Union. When I turn it on it roils and thumps and shudders and sounds like Brezhnev's armed tank division warming up in mid-winter, but when it gets going it cools the room with extraordinary speed. I look at the markings next the panel of dials and switches – all unfathomable Russian words. I bet it's never been serviced. Still works like a charm. I have even given the machine a name: Siberia.

Those Russians are baying for my blood. What is it that they think I have stolen?

I turn on the TV and there is a man being interviewed on cable news. He is a 'security analyst' apparently and he's just written a book that decries the sorry state of America. He laments the post-truth world. He berates Americans for electing a man who appeals to our emotions, our capricious loyalties and our vain tribal instincts. Somehow, it seems that they were irrational in their choice. They ought to have examined the facts, the data, and not fallen prey to their fickle, unpredictable emotional urges. He wants them all to be little computers.

I think this man – this powerful man who writes books and appears on talk shows; who has the ear of presidents and ministers of state – is a berk. He needs help.

He tells the interviewer, a man with dazzling white teeth and a squarish jaw – good-looking really, they're all good looking aren't they? – that the Age of Enlightenment is at risk; about to be subsumed by primitive emotional impulses. Can't let that happen. People – the ones who sit on their sofas, drinking beers, watching TV – are letting the whole show down. Emotions. He doesn't like them. Doesn't trust them. He insists that we pull ourselves together and adopt a 'rational world view'.

What is it to be rational? Is it rational to build nuclear weapons? Is it rational to dredge all the fossil fuels from beneath the crust of the earth and set them on fire? Not even for a dime? Is war rational? Is endless economic growth rational? Is buying more and more stuff rational? Is committing an entire lifetime to the pursuit of a monthly paycheque rational? Is sovereignty and territorial integrity rational? Borders bristling with razor wire?

What scares me is that the answer to all those questions is, yes. It's all rational. That's what you get when all you have is a rational world view; govern yourselves by the rational logic of a marketplace. It imposes a mathematically calculable price on every aspect of our experience: food, sex, pollution, even random ideas, you name it. It devalues the sick, the old, the tired, and the ignorant, which is to say, all of us and it rewards the all-knowing, eternally youthful, and supremely energetic, which is to say, none of us.

We end up not treating each other very well.

Perhaps the Enlightenment was all just make believe, after all. Yet another fanciful work of fiction – a fictional view of ourselves – that had no hope in hell of ever delivering any useful results.

And now we – the addled masses, enslaved by positive emotional feedback loops, in a decisive mood of outright rebellion, – we've elected Donald Trump – an overtly emotional creature. We see in him what we see in ourselves – the bits we don't like. A stubborn, proud, mortified human fed up with the intricacies of the Enlightened Age; the tiresome remoteness of its evermore complex rules. He's infernally pig-headed. It's compulsive viewing. He's just like us. We can't stand it and we can't stop watching – like ghouls, slowing down to gawp at the maimed on the side of the road.

A rational world is a pretend world. It's a world that makes *sense*. But it's not the world that we experience. It's not the world in which life is *lived*.

The interviewer even uses the word 'empirical' and the security analyst nods his head sagely. They all love that fucking word, those people. The commanders of the day; of the Enlightenment.

The rest of us don't know what we're about. We're the fuck ups. We like fried food. Clog the fuck out of our arteries. We pour booze down our gullets. We save up for holidays near the sea or in the mountains without really knowing why. We fuck. We jerk off. We yell and slam doors. We sob and hug. We're fucking petrified of dying. We're the fuck ups, so we take a pill and watch TV and nod here and there; we argue in bars – never really resolve anything. We hope the world will see us as normal; that we get it.

But we don't.

The security analyst is a prim man in a light-grey suit. His light-blue tie is in a perfectly symmetrical Windsor knot. He has thin lips. I imagine him sitting at the head of the table at a

Christmas lunch, surrounded by his extended family. He has a paper hat on his head and he laughs thinly at the antics of the children. Behind all that laughter he is grimacing. He is close to tears. He's crushed the life out of it, Christmas, and he can't bear it another minute.

What had Wai Ming said to me just before we said goodbye? What kind of monk do you want to be? He had said that this is a question that confronts us all. But is anyone really asking it? Or is it just the oddballs? The fringe theorists? The dream catchers?

I head down to the Destiny Pub. I need to tell John Webb that Nancy has died. He'd be interested to know, even if he is a bumptious twat.

But John isn't there.

Cindy, the barmaid says, 'He go Cambodia. He go every year, same time.'

I have a vague recollection of John visiting Cambodia the previous year and even the year before that. 'Oh yes. I suppose he does.'

Cindy seems imbued with the need to gabble. She seems to think that John is a miserly foreign nutjob. When she speaks of him I can see that she's trying to establish if I concur with that view or is she missing something?

'He go to Phnom Chisor.'

'Phnom Chisor?'

'Yeah, he go there and pray. Every time he go somewhere he say he go to pray.' She looks at me enquiringly as if to say: isn't he odd? She continues. 'He say American drop the bomb at Phnom Chisor in the wartime. Very old temple. He go pray.'

I don't know why she's telling me this or what she wants me to say.

'Mr John. He very strange, yeah?'

I nod my head. 'Yes. He's a bit strange.' I order a beer and while she pours it, I stare at myself in the mirror beyond the bar. My sideburns are distinctively grey. 'We're all a bit strange.'

A week goes by. It is a time of quiet solitude. I think a lot about Nancy. Our trip to Phou Nang Fa. I go and sit by the river in the evenings. People stroll past. They ignore me and that feels good. I stare at the river for hours – not really thinking.

Mr Lim pops in and asks me if I want my old job back.

'Yes!' I cry. 'Yes, yes, of course I do!' Once more I want to show him how utterly elated I am by the prospect.

'Ah good, good,' he says. 'You come back okay? Mr Jacques, he good boy. He good. But he young, you know? A little bit young. Staff say he a bit difficult man. I say, okay, we get Mr Juwy come back.'

I tell him that I'm massively enthusiastic and I'm well rested. I'm drinking less (which is true!) and I'm ready – indeed, *aching* – to resume my position as the general manager of the grandest hotel in the country.

He gives me a gentle pat on the back and tells me that he'll be in touch soon. I close the door behind him and I feel quite suddenly drained. Almost defeated. I lean with my back against the door and slide slowly towards the floor. Sitting with my head in my hands, I sigh deeply. No, I don't want my job back. There seem to be so few options.

When I head down to Destiny's I see John Webb in his usual

place. He's slumped on his barstool with his usual disgruntled resignation. I can't tell you how happy I am to see him. I have much to report!

First I tell him that Nancy has died.

'Oh,' he says. Again, I can tell he wants to say more: Oh no, Oh God, or Oh fuck. But he doesn't.

'She said she didn't need any heroin after all. She said she was to be carried to the end on the wings of pain. Incredible woman.'

'I guess she was.'

He doesn't want to talk about Nancy. Or people dying. Or pain.

So I switch the subject and ask him about his trip to Cambodia. 'What's with you traveling to all these little places and praying on mountain tops?

'None of your business.'

'Might not be but it's, you know, odd. Intriguing. You're a little bit mysterious.'

He looks up at me and smiles. It's almost as if I've paid him a compliment.

And then he bowls me over. He says, 'I had a past life. That's why I go to these places.'

'A past life?'

'Yes. I was a staffer in the Nixon White House. I came up with the words: *Cambodia is the Nixon Doctrine in its purest form.* That was me. I even went to Washington a few years back and sat on the grass outside the Watergate building. I knew exactly in which room the burglary had happened. I was there.'

I want to laugh out loud. But I don't.

'You were one of the burglars?'

'Not a burglar. But I went in later. Discreetly. On a clean-up mission that never produced any results.'

It all seems absurdly specific. John's jaw flexes rigidly as he ponders his past life. He seems to be taking it all very seriously.

'I don't know about past lives,' I say.

'Me too. But that's my experience. That's what I feel. I feel it strongly. What am I supposed to do? Dismiss it? Strip it of meaning? Why? Because I can't prove it?'

'Exactly,' I say. I am in wholehearted agreement with him. This might be the first time that's happened between us. 'Nixon was a fat puss,' I add.

'No two ways about it.'

17

I rub my eyes. I'm not quite sure if I'm seeing things right.

Might this be some kind of joke? Has the landlord decided to make some adjustments? Are they in the middle of a makeover?

I have just returned from the riverside. I have just watched the sunset. This has become something of a ritual over the past week. But now I am standing in my villa and I see all the armchairs in the living room have been sliced open and the innards flung about all over the floor. Curtains have been pulled from their hooks and lie in damp heaps beneath the windows. I look up. There are squarish gaps in the ceiling, like missing teeth. My heart begins to race. I run through to the study. I know exactly which ceiling board I've used to hide my Euros. It's still intact! I stand on the chair and lift it up carefully. I pat around blindly. There it is! They didn't get the money! I feel quite suddenly elated. I remove the money and stash it into my pocket.

I run upstairs. My clothing has been pulled from the cupboards. The mattress and the pillows have been cut open. In the bathroom they have squirted the toothpaste out of the tube. It's a drying green lump in the basin. The shampoo is in bright purple blotches on the shower room floor. They've sliced open the bars of soap! In the kitchen they have emptied my box of Wheatbix. They've emptied the gin and the Scotch! They've removed a pack of bacon from the freezer. It is softening on the scullery. They've emptied the contents of a washing powder container. I can see how they have sifted through it with their fingers.

I return to the study. My computer is still on. The screensaver shows me a picture of the Swiss Alps. It's been used recently. Normally the screen would have blacked out by now.

I stand in the living room. The TV has been moved too. It's at a strange angle.

'Fuck!' I say, placing my hand to my forehead. 'Fucking fuck!'

I stumble about in vague lop-sided circles, trembling, sickened by this treachery. I still feel the presence of these people; these sinister intruders.

I run outside. I have no idea what to do next. There isn't anything one *does* in this country. There is no emergency hotline. No hawkish law enforcement agency ready to swoop down and hold me to its breast. No ambulance crew to put a blanket over my shoulders and treat me with syrupy fluids for a bout of nervous shock. I stagger towards the end of the lane, not sure why.

I reach the road and peer into the street. There is no one about. Not a soul. Then I see the headlights of a car approaching at high speed. I can tell as it approaches that it is a big black modern car. I turn and start to jog back down the lane towards my house. I see my shadow caught in the headlights as it turns into the lane, following me. I start to run as fast as I can. They're going to run me down!

I reach my gate.

The car stops with hissing tyres and I hear one of the doors open.

'Julian!' a voice calls to me. It's a sort of forceful whisper.

I turn. It's Charles Brinton. He's sitting in the front passenger seat with the door open.

'You!' I cry. 'You've done this!'

'Shut up, you fool, and get in the car!'

'I … fuck you. What the fuck are you people doing to me?'

His voice has become decidedly steely; threatening. 'Shut the fuck up and get in the car.'

'Leave me alone.'

'You're in danger! Get in the fucking car!'

I stare at him. I gulp. I get in the fucking car.

Brinton has a driver. He reverses the car hurriedly down the lane. We bounce over the drain into the street and we roar off at high speed. 'Go towards the river road,' Brinton says to the driver. He turns to face me.

'What the fuck have you done? Why are you doing this to me?' I say.

'We didn't do it. Strictly speaking.'

'Strictly speaking?'

The car swerves into a busy downtown street and merges discreetly into the early evening traffic.

'It's the Americans,' he continues. 'It's their trademark. They watch too many movies you understand.'

'The Americans? What the fuck have I ever done to the Americans? Is this because I think Trump is a fat pig?'

Brinton laughs briefly and then quickly regains his usual grim expression. 'Somehow, the Russians are now convinced that you're the thief. We're not entirely sure why. We're following them and they're leading us to you. It seems there's a problem with the

CCTV surveillance footage of the night that Andropov died. And they've got prints. Your prints. They've placed you at Andropov's hotel safe. If we whisk you back to London, they'll think it's us. That's why we've told you to stay put. No sudden moves.'

'But I *didn't* steal anything from Andropov's safe! I've already told you!'

'I know. *We* know that. But the Russians don't. For all they know you could be one of us. A bullshit hotel manager, deep undercover. They're not amused.'

'But why the Americans? Why the fuck are they tearing up my house?'

'The special relationship, remember?'

'So it *was* you! You're a part of this.'

'That villa of yours is bugged to the hilt. The break-in will give the Russians pause. It's a decoy. We've bought you a bit of time.'

The car inches through the traffic and turns into the river road, Rue Fa Ngum. It is log-jammed. The neon lights of the third-grade restaurants and the seedy karaoke bars blink at us through the dimmed windows.

'You've bought me a bit of time? Time for what?'

Brinton glares at me urgently. 'Stop whining and listen. Something was stolen from Andropov's safe. This is a very serious business. It is a critical piece of information. I'm telling you more than I should but the consequences of this could be very grave. You're caught up in the middle of something that could upend the entire world order.'

'Well, fuck the world order! What about my fucking house?'

And how dare he accuse me of whining?

We drive in silence. I know I'm not going to get an answer from him.

He turns to me again. 'I assume you got your money? The Euros hidden in the ceiling?'

'How the hell do you know about that? That was a gift!'

Again, it's obvious he won't give me an answer. I slump back in the seat with a lump aching in my throat. I want to jump out of this car and run. I don't know where I'd run to, but I'd just run. Maybe into the hills. But I'm unfit and I know I couldn't run as far as the end of the street before collapsing in a great shuddering purplish heap, weeping over the sharp stabs of angina that strike my diseased chest. We move at a slow speed in this silent capsule – the whole world out there sliding past us – the ladyboys sashaying on their heels, the bored tuk-tuk drivers slouching over their handlebars, the Indian restaurateurs fanning themselves with plastic-covered menus, the tourists with their Lonely Planet guides, the women chortling amongst themselves as they sit in plastic chairs, selling barbecued entrails. I feel so far removed from that innocent chattering place; sealed up in this black car with diplomatic plates; an asset of Her Majesty's majestic government. So far removed.

I pat my pocket gently. Yes, I still have my Euros.

'We'll drop you nearby Destiny's,' Brinton says. 'Go in and have a drink. Moan away about how someone broke into your house. Return later and do your best to tidy up. Don't and I mean whatever you do, *do not* call the local police. Tell the landlord. Let him do it. Pretend you haven't a clue what this is about. You're just a lowly hotel manager who doesn't know shit, remember?'

Normally this kind of remark would have hurt. But somehow I feel a bit relieved to be reminded of my meagre status in life. I draw a strange sort of succour from my distinctive unimportance in the grand scheme of the venerated 'world order'.

'We're looking out for you, Julian. You should be grateful quite frankly.'

I don't want to say anything. I loathe Charles Brinton more than ever. I sit glumly in the back seat.

'We're doing our best to set up a new trail for the Russians. For now, just sit tight. We'll work through it. We can't have the Russians thinking it was us who nicked Andropov's stuff.'

'Oh really? So, you're not helping me. I'm helping you – while you hang me out to dry. Is that it?'

'Consider it team work,' Brinton says crisply. 'You know, we're on the same side. We're a team. That's what we do, us Brits. We work together for the common good.'

'The common good! You don't have the vaguest idea what that is. And to start with I'm not actually British. I just carry the passport.'

'Well, you should be grateful for that. Do you think the Zimbabwean government would be looking out for you as well as we are?'

'Huh! The Zimbabwean government wouldn't have gotten involved in this fucking fiasco in the first place. If I were Zimbabwean, the Russians would already be looking elsewhere. That passport you gave me is a fucking curse.'

Now it's Brinton's turn to be silent.

We pull up in a dark side street, just a few metres away from

Destiny's.

'You're a chatty little fellow, I'll give you that. Just stick to the plan. I mean it. I couldn't really care what you think of me, but it's my job to keep you alive – now *that's* a fucking curse.'

'Keeping me alive,' I say weakly. 'Why the fuck would anyone want to do that?'

Brinton turns to face me again. 'Think of Angela. That was a very touching phone call you had with her a few weeks back. Think of Angela.'

'Oh go fuck yourself, Brinton! If you had any idea of what the common good is, you'd know that listening to my phone calls isn't a part of it. Your whole thing, your system, your fucking world order is imploding in exactly the way it's supposed to implode and so you've become evermore mean-spirited, evermore pernicious, evermore … fucking ironic.'

I jump out of the car and slam the door with such ferocity that I'm a bit surprised by my strength. I even hear something rattling inside the door panelling. Good. I hope I've broken it.

The car races off and I walk around the corner to Destiny's.

It's obvious that I'm shaken, visibly so.

'Jesus!' John says. 'What's happened?'

I ignore him and order a beer.

Cindy says, 'You okay?'

'Just bring me my beer,' I say.

She turns sullenly, takes a glass and begins to fill it.

My hands are trembling and I down the beer in huge, stunning gulps. I feel inestimably better and order another.

I love my fucking booze. Not knowing.

18

I tell John everything.

I tell him about the Russians, how they removed the hard drive with the surveillance footage, how they lifted my prints off the vodka glass, how they made veiled threats and accused me of stealing some crucial artefact from Andropov's safe. I tell him about Charles Brinton and the Americans – the special relationship. They ransacked my villa. My possessions are in tatters. Brinton says my life is in danger. The entire world order is at risk. I tell him about the hotel, how I couldn't tell who is and who is not a spy. What about that Lithuanian? And the Iranian woman? Can't trust those Iranians, right?

'That old place,' John says. 'It's crawling with spies. Always has been.'

'But why? Why the Samarang? Why would this innocent little country be crawling with spies? They don't even have any oil. They're not even at war with anyone. They've been at peace for centuries.'

'It's in a geopolitically strategic location,' he says smartly.

'Geopolitically strategic? What does that even mean?'

'I have no idea.'

'I bet the whole place is bugged, though. Your hotel. From top to bottom. They'll probably just have to demolish it. The same way they dealt with the old US Embassy in Moscow.'

'Well it's absurd. I mean, the old Samarang crawling with spies!'

'You know what's interesting though?'

'What?'

'Well you've got spies from nearly every corner of the globe. Europe and North America, the Middle East and Asia. Fuck, I bet even the Australians have had look in – God knows why. You've probably even had a Chilean or two or a Cuban or a Venezuelan. They're always looking for trouble. Explains the dark glasses. But you know who's never come spying at your old hotel?'

'Who?'

'Africans.'

We both ponder this for some time. Of course, I can't be sure, but of the small number of Africans we've ever had as guests, I can't possibly imagine any of them as spies. Why not?

I put this to John.

'I can't be sure. Yes, they have their say at the General Assembly and they go to the economic summits, but when they fight it's always closer to home. It's about something immediate and proximate.'

'I rather like that.'

'Me too.'

'Here, the rest of the world, the emerging and the declining superpowers all bursting blood vessels to control the affairs of the globe and Africa can barely give a toss.'

'Not a toss. So it would seem.'

'It's almost as if they know something, like, for instance, none of this geopolitical stuff really means anything.'

'Well, let's face it. Those African nations, those nation-states, they're not really nations at all. They're just leaky colonial relics, modest political structures with whom we can deal, with whom we can sign treaties: oil and gas, uranium, security pacts, fly-over rights, arms deals. We can taunt them with sanctions and development money – our diplomatic panoply of carrots and sticks. But they enjoy scant legitimacy amongst Africa's people – the ones who are supposed to matter. It's why they're always so shaky, so massively corrupt. You get your rebel groups, your gangster states, your presidents for life – trying to keep it together or break it apart, whichever way the wind blows.'

'You mean all the war? All those African wars?'

'Sure. You know the single deadliest conflict so far this century? You think it's Syria or Yemen or the Rohingyas? Not even close. It's the Congo. Four million dead and it's barely made a ticker tape.'

I ponder this for some time. What does this mean? This African experience that no one really wants to talk about?

John continues, 'You want to know the difference between Asia and Africa?'

I nod with a smile.

'In Africa, if they want to rob you, they'll hit you over the head with a stick. In Asia they'll just smile.'

I laugh.

'Each approach has its benefits,' he adds. 'In Africa, at least you know where you stand and in Asia you don't get hit over the head with a stick.'

'And us? Us whites, Westerners or whatever it is that we call ourselves?'

'Oh, we're the biggest joke of all. We've insisted on a set of written rules that determine when our violent urges and deceptive airs will and will not be tolerated. It has become a vast and complex piece of work and relies on a vast and complex bureaucracy. So we obsess over governance, the business of governing and being governed. We agonize over the fortunes of politicians, the ones charged with making the rules. But rules, static and unbending by nature, operate in a permanent state of failure and are in need of permanent reform. We've all become exasperated. Society, the whole idea of it, has become nothing more than a kind of tyranny. So, all we have left is the individual. Individuals running around arguing over their rights. We no longer belong to communities. We belong to protest movements. Ready to throttle each other over whose rights should prevail. We're a stubborn lot, still enamoured by the illusory thrill of a *final solution*. And we've marketed this folly to young people all over the world.'

'And the oldies of Africa look on.'

'Africa looks on. Heartbroken.'

'The Mother Continent.'

John pauses and smiles at me. 'Nice image.'

We end up playing pool. John loses. Time and time again. I can see his angst every time I sink the black. But he leans on his cue, sucks aggressively on a cigarette and says, 'Let's play another one.'

19

I have a dream. I'm down at the river, just at the foot of Phou
Nang Fa. We are on the edge of the pebble river bed. There are a
lot of people about. We've arrived in various cars, tourist buses
even. I don't know who they are. I see this woman sitting in a
wheelchair at some distance from me. I can't really see her clearly.
I think it's Nancy, but I'm not really sure. I call to all the people.
'Hey! Look, I'm going to show you how it's done. It's really quite
easy.' They all murmur amongst each other with a vague sort
of anticipation. Or is it apprehension? I strip off my shirt and
slip off my shoes. But I become rather coy about removing my
pants. 'It's okay,' I say. I walk towards the water's edge. Looking
downstream, I see Wai Ming and John Webb sitting on the rock
that juts out over the stream. Wai Ming appears not to notice me
but John has his hands cupped around his mouth and he's yelling
something at me, but I hear no words. He seems a bit frantic.
I turn to the crowd behind me. 'Here goes!' I seem mightily
proud of myself and I submerge myself in the water. Somehow
my trousers have disappeared and I know that I'm completely
naked. I dip my head under, just as I had done before, while my
arms reach out upstream clutching onto a rock. But the water
is far more powerful than I had expected. It is fierce. I look up,
gasping. I'm in a roaring muddy torrent. I catch a glance of a few

people standing on the edge. They all look mortified! They have their hands to their mouths. They collectively groan in horror as I struggle against the muscular force of the water. I let go of the rock. I am swept away, pummelled and bruised over the rocks, and every now and then I find a little air.

And the most terrifying part of the dream is when I wake. I am drenched. I am gasping for air. It's as if the dream will not let go of me. I feel it again. A great torrent of water splashing over my head. I blink and I see the Russian standing in front of me. One of his henchmen stands next to him, holding a bucket.

'That's enough,' the Russian says. 'He's awake.'

I cough and splutter and sit up. My body aches. I shake my head. I'm half real, half dream. I can't tell which is which.

I'm sitting on one of my mutilated armchairs in the living room. It's soaked. The tiled floor glimmers dimly in a pool of water. I'm shirtless, but still have my trousers on. I surreptitiously pat my thigh. Yes, the money is still in my pocket. Wet, but still there.

Looking down at the floor with my head in my hands I say, 'What? What the fuck do you want?'

The Russian takes a step closer to me. I can feel his shadow hanging over me.

'You're quite a little actor, Mr Lockhardt. No more games, yes? You know very well why we're here. Come now,' he laughs stiffly, 'you must surely have been expecting us, no?'

I look up to face him. He is a tall man with distinctive jowls and a pinched mouth. A creepy fucker if ever there was one.

'No. I wasn't expecting you.'

He turns to his cohort and says, 'Fill up the bucket. It seems as if he hasn't fully woken.'

'Oh enough with the fucking bucket! Jesus! Of course, I'm awake!'

I try to stand but the Russian pushes me back down into the chair. My heart begins to race. I look out towards the window. It is light grey outside. Still early morning. Before sunrise.

'Well now, let's keep this nice and simple, shall we, Mr Lockhardt?' There is a strange note of affability in his voice now.

He turns away and says to his cohort, 'Bring poor Mr Lockhardt a towel. Poor man has been having a wet dream!'

The two of them laugh uproariously.

'How do you know about my dreams?' I snap at them.

This question rather flummoxes them. It's not what they're expecting. The short fat one trudges off to the kitchen in search of a towel. No, they don't really want to talk about dreams. That was a just a little joke. A little Russian joke.

The man lights a cigarette. 'Just give us the flash drive, Mr Lockhardt. That's all we're here for. It couldn't be simpler.' He exhales sternly.

'Do you mind telling me who you are? I mean, your name?'

'Of course!' he smiles brightly. 'That's very rude of me. I am Dimitri. Dimitri Mikov. Pleased to make your acquaintance.'

I need an aspirin.

'Look, I need an aspirin. I have a headache. Can't think straight. Let me get myself an aspirin,'

Dimitri lifts his head slightly and calls to the kitchen in Russian. I detect the word 'aspirin'.

'Tell him they're upstairs in the bathroom cabinet.'

I hear the little one trudging up the old wooden staircase to the bathroom.

'I don't have a flash drive, Dimitri. Never have had one. I'm not good with computers.'

'You're making this very difficult. Let me set out a few important facts. You might want to change your mind. You see, we have completed our investigation of Mr Andropov's death. We have direct evidence that you accessed the safe in his room. You had the master code, yes? We have the surveillance tape that shows you going into the room after he died. You went in alone. No witnesses. We took the surveillance footage, as you will recall, and we asked you if any copies were made. Do you recall?'

I nod, slightly exhausted by the man's voice.

'And you said no, no copies. But our analysis shows this to be untrue. Worse still is that there are 37 minutes of tape that are missing. We logged our removal of the server at 09.35. But the tape stops at 08.58. So, it seems that you have lied to us Mr Lockhardt. Nothing could be plainer. And let me add, I don't like to be lied to. It upsets me.'

'Well I still don't have your flash drive, Dimitri.'

'If you keep lying to me, Mr Lockhardt, this isn't going to end well.'

'Oh, I see. Is this when you strap me to this chair? Start pulling out my fingernails? Electrocuting my balls? I suppose I'm the kind of man who'd cave under that sort of pressure. In fact, I know I am. I suppose, at best, I'd have to make something up; lie to you. I'd had have to do the very thing that upsets you.'

'Oh, please don't be so melodramatic my friend. We're not torturers. We're diplomats from the embassy. We don't pull out fingernails. Please, a little, how do you say, decorum?'

His fat colleague waddles down the stairs with a glass of water and a tab of aspirin. I swallow the aspirin hungrily and down the water. I hand the glass back to him. 'Please. Another.'

He seems annoyed but Dimitri nods calmly, assenting to my request and the man hurries away to fetch me more water.

'But then again, even if we keep your fingernails in place, Mr Lockhardt, we do have certain ways of securing your co-operation. I mean, think of Angela, yes? And the little one. Marcus, is it? Think of how sad it would be if things didn't work out so well.'

'What the fuck are you saying? This is the work of diplomats? You're fucking thugs, the lot of you.'

Just then we are both startled to hear another voice from the doorway.

'I'd hardly think that's an appropriate way to address a Russian diplomat, Julian.' Stepping in through the front doorway is Charles Brinton.

He nods at Dimitri. 'Good to see you Dimitri.' He nods at me too. 'Julian.' I am a bedraggled British subject, soaked on a torn sofa in a ransacked house. 'Can't say I like what you've done to the place,' he adds.

Behind Charles is one of his goons. He stands at the door with his arms folded. He is, I'm rather relieved to note, a lot bigger than Dimitri's rotund, wheezing companion. Charles turns to Dimitri, 'And I can't say that this is an appropriate way to address a British subject either. This whole conversation seems to be rather uncivil.'

'What the hell are you doing here?' Dimitri scowls.

'I'm looking out for one of our citizens. Isn't that the work of us diplomats, after all? Can't have him dragged out of here into a van with blackened windows, thrown into some subterranean cell of that monstrous concrete embassy of yours now, can we?'

'We're not in that kind of business, Mr Brinton.'

'Really? Do you honestly think anyone trusts the Russians anymore? You've lost the trust of the world. And gained what, one might ask?'

Dimitri laughs. 'You and your fake news.'

'And you and yours.'

I start to realise what an utterly puerile exchange this is turning out to be. I feel like smacking both men across the lips. They're starting to infuriate me.

Mercifully, for all of us, we all hear the sound of a big car, its tyres screeching to a smoky halt outside my gate.

It's the two Americans! The folks from the Church of Jesus Christ of Latter Day Saints. Or the Seventh Day Adventists. Or Episcopalians or whatever they are. Remember them? Harrison Ford and Ben Affleck? Of course! They're CIA! I feel like a perfect fool for not having spotted that earlier!

Charles appears to be outraged. 'I thought we agreed …' he stammers and blanches.

But Harrison interrupts him. 'We'll take it from here,' he says smoothly. I've heard that line in so many movies – so many squabbles between competing law enforcement officers over who has *jurisdiction* – I almost want to laugh out loud.

Dimitri's helper stands in the kitchen doorway – a forlorn figure – helplessly holding my glass of water.

'I'll have that now, please. Actually, could you get me another one? I'm parched. Bit of a heavy night last night.'

He hands me the glass and slopes towards the kitchen to get me another. Not bad service … for a thug.

Harrison Ford says, 'Look, gentlemen, the fact that we're all standing here proves one thing and one thing only. The flash disk isn't here.'

'You mean flash drive,' says Dimitri.

'Actually, it's a flash stick,' Charles offers.

'Whatever the fuck it's called, it's not here.'

'And how do you reach that conclusion?' says Dimitri. 'How do you explain Mr Lockhardt's lies about the copies of the tape, his fingerprints on the cupboard door that contained Andropov's safe?'

'I don't need to explain anything,' the American says. 'I'm American, remember.'

The Russian helper is carrying another glass of water from the kitchen. Harrison Ford says, 'Actually, I'll have one of those too if you don't mind.'

'Me too,' adds Ben Affleck.

The Russian hands me my glass and turns with a heavy stoop back to the kitchen.

Harrison wipes his brow. 'The sun's not even up and it's already ninety degrees.'

'Thirty-three degrees,' says Charles crisply.

'Well at least we don't drive on the left side of the road,'

Harrison sneers and Dimitri smiles too.

'It's not the left side. It's the right side. You don't know right from wrong anymore that's your problem,' Charles says caustically.

'So much for the special relationship,' Dimitri chimes.

I can't take it anymore.

'Enough!' I shout. I stand up. My back aches. 'This is my fucking house you morons and you ... you ...'

I pause for quite a long time and it surprises me that no one interrupts.

'You people have no idea what you're even arguing about. Fahrenheit or Celsius? Flash stick or flash drive? Or maybe its access to oil. Or shipping lanes. Or emerging markets. Perhaps it's even the supremacy of an idea. The preservation of some kind of loosely defined *way of life*. Is that what gets you the license to kill? The assassinations? The blacklists and no-fly zones? The spheres of influence and the collateral damage? What are you people anyway? The guardians of national security? Willing to give your very own lives for the nation state? Bully for you! And willing to take lives too, I suppose; to stand here in my upturned house and push me around. Well there are plenty of reasons to behave like an arsehole. It doesn't just have to be in the name of your country. It could be a sports club, a religion, a language, a brand, a fucking menu or a taste for wearing an unusual hat. You can hide behind anything if you choose to; anything except the way you see yourself. And nothing disgusts us more than that. Everything else is just a game: your race, your nation, even your very own name. It's all a mock-up.'

'You're a very naïve man, Mr Lockhardt,' says Harrison Ford. 'I'm not going to stand here and listen to a lecture about world peace. People aren't to be trusted and that's all there is to it.'

'So let's monitor the poor bastards! Let's scrutinize everything they do and whack them if they step out of line. Haven't any of you read that book? *1984*? I'm not saying I have, but I've seen the movie and it's a fucking horror story. You're not building trust. You're giving in. You're giving in to the worst of humanity. This whole global superstructure of yours, it's not about people. It's about power. You give us a flag and a song and we get to watch the motorcade, to revel in the power of the state; to feel its fleeting glory. This, you tell us, is our freedom. But it's just a mock-up. There's nothing really there.'

These men, these spymasters, each imbued with love of country, their hollow societies, they look so tired, so drained of pluck! I'd seen that look before, when Nancy had first checked in and had finally consented to the suite with no view of the stupa.

'You probably all know that my friend, Nancy, has just died. She'd been sick for a long time with cancer. I'd never known a person who understood what freedom was until I met her. She was free of her very own name. The decay, the darkness, the disease had shaped her into a person ...' My voice begins to wobble. I pause and breathe and soldier on. 'She was a person I can only admire. And let me tell you, I haven't admired anyone for a very long time.'

I point outside the window and note the first glimmer of dawn through the trees.

'You know in these little places? These people know what

it's like not to be trusted. They know how things go wrong; how things can get ugly. Do you think that's breaking news? But they're not bombing the earth in the name of freedom. Freedom is not given to us by the state. It's something that we give to each other. But you lot! You dare not trust a man. You dare not even *be* trusted. You trust only in the rules, the restrictions, and policy prescriptions. You expect of us nothing more than machine-like obedience. Your hatred of humanity, your hatred of this horrid earth has completely overwhelmed you. All your bosses can do is try to mollify us with a tax cut or a bit of government spending. Dither over who has the money and who doesn't. Trade routes and capital markets. What an impoverished view you have of humanity, of people, of what it is to live!'

I pause. I breathe heavily. The sad fat Russian helper quietly deposits the two glasses of water on the table and places his hands on his hips, listening to me intently – as are the others.

I resume in a quieter voice. 'What, might I ask is even on Andropov's flash stick or drive or disk? The nuclear codes? Here you all are ready to slaughter each other and, I might add, a perfectly innocent hotel manager, just to make sure that your nation – your petty-minded idea of nationhood – is the one that gets to blow up the world. You can't talk to me about freedom if you've given up on people, given up on our stories. You're all deranged; deranged by conventional wisdom.'

Now I want them all to leave.

But Dimitri says, 'I have no idea what you're talking about, Mr Lockhardt. Perhaps you're still a bit hung-over. Fine, maybe we don't trust each other – nice to have this talk in a bar somewhere

– but right now, what counts is that I don't trust you!'

And then a strangely familiar voice calls from outside. 'Oh, you can trust him! You can trust Mr Julian!'

In walks Mr Saudi. He's perspiring as usual and wearing one of his trademark silk shirts. He grins at us. 'I have the tape!' he says with a hopeful gleam in his narrow eyes. 'You see, Mr Lockhardt has been set up!' He draws from his pocket a flash drive. I immediately recognize it. It's the copy of the surveillance tape that Jacques had shown me after the Russians stormed in and removed the server.

'It seems that Mr Lockhardt wasn't the only one to enter Andropov's room after he died.' He turns to me. 'Mr Julian? You have your laptop here?'

I run into my study and am eagerly followed by the seven international spies. I plug in the flash drive.

'Fast forward it to 08.58,' says Mr Saudi. I wonder how that fat little man might have got hold of the tape. Was this the culmination of hours of seductive pillow talk between him and Sam the barman?

I fast forward the tape and there it is! About three minutes after I disappear down the corridor, Jacques arrives from the direction of the service elevator. He has his back to the camera. He stops outside Room 515, his head assiduously facing the floor.

'That's Jacques!' I cry.

He enters the room. He is in there for all of six minutes. He returns to the corridor, straightens his jacket, closes the door and hurriedly strides back towards the service elevator. He has, unfortunately, dropped his guard and looks directly at the camera, before hurrying on.

'Jacques?' Dimitri says, looking at his fellow spies.

They're all nonplussed. No idea who Jacques is.

'He's my assistant manager. He's French!' I say delightedly.

They all rush towards the door.

'Sorry about ripping up the place,' Harrison Ford says and Ben Affleck gives me a sympathetic nod.

They all push and elbow each other to get through the front door.

In the midst of this scuffle, Charles Brinton turns to Mr Saudi. 'You arrived a bit late. You missed Julian's speech. It was rather good!' He turns to me and says, 'You old colonial orphan!' He winks and pushes Mr Saudi out of the way.

They jump into their various diplomatic vehicles, and head for the Samarang at high speed.

Jacques! Smug little prick!

20

Do you want to know where I am now?

Well, I never returned to the Samarang. Mr Lim had implored me to resume my role as the general manager, even offered me a pay increase, quite a substantial one, but I said no.

Jacques, so it turned out, was the mysterious Israeli to whom Charles Brinton had referred. He wasn't even French! By the time they all arrived at the hotel, Jacques had already left – taken a flight to Bangkok and from there, who knows? So far, the consequences of his malfeasance have not yet been felt – by that I mean that no one has blown up the world, Donald Trump is still the president of America, the war in Syria still grinds on. Maybe they got him. Maybe he landed up dead, his body in the trunk of a black Mercedes parked on the banks of Lake Geneva. The critical data – so it seems – never fell into the 'wrong' hands after all.

I still feel a bit troubled that I never took Jacques for a spy. The theory that emerged later – disclosed to me by Charles Brinton as we took a drink in a bar – was that he was a rogue agent. The Samarang, as the leading hotel in a country of strategic geopolitical importance, was riddled with spies – just as John Webb had surmised. Jacques had known about Andropov's nefarious willingness to trade state secrets that ought to have been kept close to the breast of Mother Russia. He'd never worked at the Marriott in Paris. He was simply an Israeli with a flawless French accent. Deep undercover, one might say.

So, no I didn't return to the Samarang.

Where am I now? I am on the banks of the Phou Nang Fa river. Quite some distance downstream from where Nancy, Wai Ming and I had visited.

With the money gifted to me by Nancy, I took a twenty-year lease of some paddy land and built a few wooden bungalows on stilts. The river roars past day and night, inky in the moonlight and shimmering silver in the daylight. She is a garrulous young thing, free at last from the rocky caverns deep in the breast of the mother mountain, bubbling over the smooth rocks, seeking that place along its twisting course to the sea where height and depth begin and end.

My little place is a refuge for backpackers mostly. I have stuck to my promise – the promise that I made when my brother and I had shared that room back at the Leopard Rock Hotel in the middle of the Bunga Forest in my old Rhodesia: I'd take care of people when they're away from home. This is a place – just one small place on planet earth – where someone will take care of you.

I can't even begin to tell you what ripping reviews I get on TripAdvisor. They take tubes down the river. They go hiking through the forest in search of caves near the limestone karsts. They sit on mats on the floor of the main verandah and play cards. They listen to transcendental music on their headphones and sometimes they get rid of those altogether and listen to the cicadas and the frogs and the occasional warbled call of the rain birds.

I cook for them. I am inspired in my kitchen. I can hardly believe myself. Sautéed mushrooms with fresh-ground herbs, beef fillet fried with cracked pepper, crushed ginger and a pinch of chilli powder and served in thin translucent slices alongside piquant forest herbs. Sapodilla fruits with homemade vanilla ice cream and fresh-ground cinnamon. You name it. I'm so excited in the kitchen, so consumed by the process of cooking that sometimes my guests have to wait. Some of them complain, but they eat their words when I place the food on their table with a flourish! I can't tell you what this means to me – each plate of food.

I also work in the garden. There is a small plantation of teak trees neighbouring my plot. In the shade I have planted wild ginger and I have lined the pathways with small hedges of miniature hibiscus. And yes, I have fuchsia, frangipani and bougainvillea dotted about the place – not so that I might be reminded of the function rooms of the grand old Samarang, but so that the Samarang may, in some mysterious way, be conscious of these plants that grow and die here in this garden. Dragonflies dip and flutter in the slanting light, lizards bask in the sun. The garden has its share of symbols too. I used a tractor to haul a large rock from the river. It's a well-rounded, gold-coloured rock. There is a slight dent in the surface which collects a bit of rainwater. The water is important because at the foot of the rock, in the shade of ferns I have planted, is a little plaque that says: She taught them how to swim.

And there is also an even bigger rock, still on the riverbank – a ginormous thing that watches over the spirited flow of the river. This I call the Leopard Rock – it reminds me of the life of my brother; our excitement when we shared our own room at the first hotel we ever stayed in.

And I also have a small rock near the entrance to the dining room – which itself is a simple wooden balcony next to the river. The rock is dark granite with intricate white veins. I have a small plaque there too which says: What kind of monk do you want to be?

I am grateful to the people of this little country for letting me stay here. I have a visa – all the right paperwork – and I get to renew it once a year. As far as I can tell, so long as I don't behave like a fat puss, they'll let me stay here forever. This seems fair. And I commend myself for not behaving like a fat puss.

And I have grown to love this land, not for its impressive scenery or its discreetness on a world stage crammed with bumptious actors, but for its people. It is perhaps their innate awareness that life is very hard. This awareness binds each of them from the day of their birth, in a bad house, to the day of their death, in a good house, and it grants them a resilience too many of us have abandoned in favour of fickle promises of happiness.

And do you know that Pon (yes, the same Pon from the Destiny Pub) has followed me up here and she helps out? No, we're not lovers. Not even close. But I do love her. I love her very much. She is my translator, my general manager, my liaison with the tax authorities (yes, the adage about death and taxes is true) and in the mornings, she is accompanied by some of the girls from the local village and they go off into the forest to find herbs and mushrooms and wild honey. And you wouldn't believe that Pon is a bit of a whizz on the computer. So she helps manage all the online bookings.

Still, she doesn't say much. She's a quiet, contemplative young thing. Sometimes I envy her.

Even John Webb pops in every now and again. He sits on the balcony drinking his aperitif (he's brings his own) and leans forward over the table, scribbling notes into one of his many notebooks which are stacked up high next to him.

'You know,' he says. He looks up at me through the hatch into the kitchen. 'I once knew a guy. He was a nuclear scientist. Very well respected. Advised presidents. And we got chatting in an airport bar. Now, I mean, I have to stress, this guy was super well-respected. And he was feeling a bit morose and he explained to me that he suffered from an unfortunate condition. And I said: oh yeah? And he said: yeah, I suffer from something called lysdexia. And I said: don't you mean dyslexia? And he shook his head firmly and said; no, no, no it's lysdexia. Look it up. It's in the dictionary under "d".'

We both laugh.

He says, 'You'll never convince anyone of anything very important. You might move them for a while, provoke or inspire them – the way that those corporate motivational speakers do, novelists do – but soon enough we slot back into our old positions, utterly distraught that no one sees the world in the same way we do.'

John takes a final slug of his Pastis and pours himself another.

I look at him quizzically for a while and say, 'I'm going to put a rock in the garden for you too'.

'Me?'

'Yes. When you finally publish a novel.'

'Huh. I'll sooner be buried *under* a rock.'

John was being unnecessarily self-deprecating. He did publish his first novel a few months later. It was called *Lisp*. The opening line: *Why did they put an 's' in the word lisp? Unfortunate oversight? Or was it something more deliberate?* I deposited a knobbly weathered grey stone beneath a sturdy young banyan tree. It reads: Pray on a mountain top.

Rock, in itself, whether it is placed in my garden by my own hand or whether or not accompanied by some sort of inscription, serves to remind me of the power of the earth, its constant resilience in the face of all those who live and die on it shifting surface.

It's not possible to see Phou Nang Fa mountain from here. She is at least a four-hour drive away. I have a Soviet-made army jeep built in the 50s. It's rather fetchingly called a Ulyanovsky Avtomobilny Zavod. The marketing people pulled out all the stops with that one! I've installed a minibar in the back. Sometimes I take folks out to the spot where Nancy once sat contemplating her imminent mortality. I do not mention this to visitors but they love the journey and like to swim in the stream. Sometimes, in the faces of some of them, I see that something moves them there.

It's true that people aren't always to be trusted. Some of the guests deliberately complain about the food, just to get out of paying for it. Some have even snuck out in the early morning to avoid the hotel bill. These backpackers are an indigent lot. One even stole the towels from the room and then placed a nasty review online, saying it's the worst hotel in the world. And still, that isn't really any of my business. If it hurts, I suppose that's good enough.

And do you know that I still smoke and drink? But not as much as I used to. And I never smoke with the deliberate intention of contracting cancer. The prospect of dying in that way properly appals me. Now, I am motivated by a sort of curious intrigue; a fascination over what it is to live here on earth, seized at once by euphoria and despondency, through the dreaming spaces, the shadow and light, the diseased and fragrant forest through which my river travels. It is, I suppose, little more than an abiding interest in seeing how the story ends.

Best bad movie I ever watched: you've got to see how the story ends.

Now I am chopping red onions. With one deft manoeuvre I slide the finely chopped pieces into a smoking hot wok. Slightly asphyxiated – pleasingly so – by a plume of fizzing smoke and steam I toss the onions with a spatula and prepare to add the chillies and chunks of galangal to the wok. I hear Pon checking in a new guest on the other side of the hatch. It seems as if there is a bit of a disagreement. The new guest – a woman – speaks with distinctive forcefulness. I am reminded of Nancy. Perhaps this woman wants a view of the stupa. Well, she'll be out of luck. We don't have a stupa around here. We only have a view of the river.

Then I detect her accent! She's a South African! I hear the sound of a child. He seems to be whining and the woman tells him to be quiet. I can't quite contain my curiosity and I step out of the kitchen and stand behind Pon's small check-in counter. I see the woman and her child and they both stare at me as if I'm some kind of apparition – a slightly mesmerizing, ghost-like figure in a grubby apron, holding a spatula. She is younger than her voice suggested. She has jet-black hair, slightly tanned skin and a small dark freckle on her upper lip. She has a gentle curve to her nose and a long slender neck. The boy has jet-black hair too. And the same tanned skin. He is a lanky kid and he holds onto his mother's arm, leaning against her as if disinclined to ever let her go.

We look at each other for a long time. I recognize her, of course. But I stand mutely, smelling of onions, without anything to say. I look at the boy and he clutches onto his mother even more tightly. I return to face her and I see her top lip begin to curl and quiver – just the way it used to when she was little. Tears slide down her cheeks.

Angela and Marcus stay with me for two weeks.

I cook breakfast for them every morning and I take it through to their room. Marcus goes out with Pon and the girls into the forest. He returns ebullient, with the front of his T-shirt folded up, full of mushrooms. I take him on a wooden long-tail boat down the river. We tootle through the dappled fringes and the delight on his face must surely mirror the delight on my own. We sit on the Leopard Rock and catch fish with bamboo rods. In the evenings he helps me make a fire in a pit in the garden and we roast strips of pork and vegetables on skewers. I take them to the caves near the limestone peaks. There are the remnants of old offerings at the entrances to the caves – burnt-out joss sticks, patches of blackened wax, the dry withered heads of marigolds.

'They come to pray here,' I say. 'They crawl under – into – this old earth, take refuge in her darkest spaces and they pray.'

Angela tells me that she no longer works for Big Pharma. She tells me that she did eventually recall her childhood games and how she loved to play the nurse. So now she works in the pharmacological department of an academic hospital. Not as much money, but it's better work. And she is married to Sean. She shows me photos of the wedding. 'It's not so much the wedding that counts or even the idea of getting married,' she says. 'It's just the possibility that two people make a promise; a promise to take care of each other. Somehow, that's made a difference, not only to us, but to how we see the world.'

'Right,' I say.

And she tells me that Maureen has emphysema. Stage two. I gulp. I light a cigarette. I put it out again. 'It's a struggle all right.'

'She sends her love. She says she thinks about you all the time.' There is a long pause and she adds. 'She asked me to ask you if you still remember the Datsun parked near the beach, when you both listened to Katrina and the Waves.'

I sigh deeply. This pains me more than I expected. 'Love,' I say. 'It's almost annoying that people are capable of such a thing. It'd almost be better if we were just like cows, mooching along, aimlessly following one another, mooing at each other without meaning.'

Angela laughs. 'Almost,' she says.

'Yes. Almost.'

I can't quite stand the idea that they'll be leaving soon. As the day of their departure looms ever closer, like a creeping afternoon shadow, I find myself drifting towards a state of blithering panic. A shadow indeed.

On the day before their departure, I pack the Ulyanovsky Avtomobilny Zavod with lunch. I stock the mini-bar with beers.

I stand with Marcus, waiting for Angela. He holds onto my arm, leans on me in the same way that he leans against his mother. To feel this kid holding on to my arm, as if for dear life – to feel this – is to live. This is where the meaning is. I've never been more aware of this in all my life.

'I hope you come back again. You tell your mother, okay? You tell her that you want to come and visit grandpa and you come back and visit. Okay?'

He looks up at me and nods. He blinks and seems a bit perplexed by my desperation.

Angela emerges from her room.

'Okay, we're all set!' I say.

We climb into the jeep. After my typical struggle with the gear lever, the clang and clash of the cogs, and a belch of purple smoke from the exhaust, we set off for the hills.

'Where are we going, grandpa?' says Marcus.

'I've got something to show you!' I say. 'We're going to a mountain. It's a huge mountain. She has great big eyes and she has a gentle smile on her face. She rests and she stirs. Sometimes she even gets a bit cross. And sometimes, if you look closely, she'll even give you a wink.'

He laughs at the idea of it.